THE
AVENGERS
ANEW

Editors John Doyle and Alan Samson

Published by
Michael Joseph Ltd
44 Bedford Square
London WC1

First published 1985

British Library Cataloguing in Publication Data
Rogers, Dave
Avengers anew
1. Avengers, The (Television Programme)
I. Title
791.45'72 PN1992.77.A9

ISBN 0-7181-2604-1

Produced by John Doyle
Typesetting and Prints by Bloomsbury Graphics, London WC1
Printed in Britain by
Purnell & Sons (Book Production) Ltd
Bristol, Avon

Cover photograph from 'Town of No Return'
Backcover photograph from 'Honey for the Prince'

CONTENTS

ACKNOWLEDGEMENTS

Thanks are due to the following individuals and organisations for their cordial help during the preparation of this volume.

In particular, Bud Payton, of EMI, who never failed to lend an ear to my countless requests (and without whom ...). David Semple and Bernard Heywood (both of EMI), who always found time to help. Jack Breckon and his staff of Thames Television. Albert Fennell and Brian Clemens, whose inspired work formed the basis for this volume. Dick Blayney of Eurotel Distribution. The Brookes family (Josie, Lewis and Carl) for their unfailing support. Colin Bayley of The Place Bookshop. Friends Stephen & Joy Curry, Bill Bradshaw (UK). David Caruba & Dan Recchia (USA). Not forgetting: Ian Beard, Ron Hood (UK) and Dave Schleicher (USA) for their help with the merchandise section, William Carty for the loan of his photographs, and Angie and Jackie of R.A. Waspe Ltd (Burslem).

I would also like to thank John Doyle for producing this volume and retaining faith in the product, and Jennie Davies of Michael Joseph for her continued support.

Finally, a big thank you to my wife Celia (who showed her expertise by cross-referencing the alphabetical list of actors and actresses), my daughter Leah, son Stephen and my mum, who made it all possible.

This book is respectfully dedicated to everyone who appeared in/wrote for/directed/produced/designed costumes for/or swept the studio floor during those heady days spent producing *The Avengers,* and, in particular, one man. A real life toff – Patrick Macnee.

BY

DAVE ROGERS

A FANTASTIC STORY TOLD BY AN EXTRAORDINARY FAN

MICHAEL JOSEPH

FOREWORD BY PATRICK MACNEE

I am delighted to introduce *Avengers Anew* by Dave Rogers, whose first book on *The Avengers* was so comprehensive and entertaining.

To have been part of *The Avengers* in the Sixties was an experience which, at the time, took many different courses. It actually started as a live television show with Ian Hendry for three months until it was taped. In October 1961 there was a five-month actors' strike during which Ian went off to become a movie star, leaving us without anybody to play the lead. When the series started again I was still available (possibly because I couldn't get a job anywhere else!) and they had these scripts already written for Ian Hendry. Suddenly, Sydney Newman of ABC Television had the bright idea of casting a woman in the part, so Honor Blackman was introduced to play the man's role. This happened to coincide with the emergence of women's lib and she became a cult figure and a dramatic contrast to me; I was really playing myself – or at least one of my forebears in modern dress.

We were an unlikely couple who, for some extraordinary reason, caught the public's fancy. In 1963 we won the Variety Artistes Award for the Best Television Personalities of that year and I think we managed to create – not just we two but the whole of the *Avengers* team – something that was a little unique.

We continued smoothly for a couple of years and then they decided to put the series on film instead of tape. At this time Honor left us to play with James Bond in *Goldfinger* and we spent a further nine months trying to get the filmed series together. In retrospect, it seems to me that even as far back as the Ian Hendry days – in fact because of Ian – the quality of the shows was far higher than anything in England at that time. Of course, it helped that they were done with extraordinary ingenuity because we were able to use the finest directors, designers and writers in that field. There was something special about those early Blackman shows. I don't know if they stand up now, but the insouciance, bohemianism, originality of approach and attitude of those early programmes was, in my view, never quite recaptured.

We then began filming a further twenty-six black-and-white stories with a golden jewel of an actress who alighted upon us like a glorious butterfly on a summer's day and proceeded to add gossamer to the show. Allied to her incredible technique was great charm and warmth. Her name was, of course, Diana Rigg.

When Diana left the show she was succeeded by Linda Thorson, a most bounteous and delightful woman. Then the series went to bed and Linda and I were shot into space, apparently never to be heard of again. But somebody wanted to make a commercial in 1975 for champagne and they thought that Linda Thorson – a particular favourite in France at that time – would be a great draw. They also wondered, 'Who was that man who shared those adventures with all those girls?' They contacted me at the prestigious Chichester Theatre Company and we made the commercial, which led to a French producer coming up and asking if I wanted to do *The Avengers* again. After a while I said yes. We did *The New Avengers* and 'discovered' Joanna Lumley – one of the most beautiful women in the United Kingdom and certainly one of the brightest – and Gareth Hunt, who we already knew to be a very fine actor.

It has become the fashion to denigrate *The New Avengers* – to say it wasn't as good as the old. Well perhaps it wasn't. But on the other hand they were twenty-six highly original thrillers, with the new concept of a *threesome*. It *could* have worked really well but many consider it didn't. The reason perhaps is that it wasn't fully developed. They used me as the known factor in it and they tried to launch two new young people. Arguably they should have either used myself and Diana Rigg or started completely anew and used Joanna Lumley and Gareth Hunt on their own – without the hindrance of the father-figure alongside.

One other aspect that I feel is of interest is how far we preceded almost any show of its type. We started filming long before the first James Bond film came out – though not, of course, before the *books* came out. I think, if I were really honest, that *The Avengers* owes a very strong debt to the Ian Fleming books, and in fact when I was approached to do the part I was advised by director Don Leaver to read them. Unfortunately I found their attitude towards casual violence and their male chauvinism extremely unpleasant. Consequently I took the veneer of Bond for Steed without using the core. In other words, what I left out were the words 'licence to kill'. I had no licence to kill. All I really had as Steed was a will to bring the enemy to book, so to speak, and I like to feel that I could go out without a gun and use whatever was to hand. The umbrella was simply a symbol: not of authority or the mighty power of the gun, but a means of concealing gadgets, – which again, of course, was pure Bond.

These are just a few observations and I bless you and thank you for having supported over the years the cult that became *The Avengers*. Enjoy *Avengers Anew*.

Patrick Macnee

Patrick Macnee as Steed, a Queen's Messenger in Death Dispatch. *John Steed, the undercover man who cloaks his activities behind the façade of a wealthy man-aboout-town. This is an unusual shot of Steed. After this early episode he developed the more familiar, debonair, bowler-hatted image.*

INTRODUCTION

It was a time when twenty cigarettes could be bought for 20p; a pint of beer cost 12p; petrol cost 25p a gallon; and viewers could watch their favourite programmes on a television set rented for a fraction over 44p per week.

An era when 'heroes' were television's staple diet and female viewers drooled as Roger Moore donned his Simon Templar halo to rescue damsels in distress; Patrick 'Danger Man' McGoohan meted out rough justice to saboteurs and foreign dictators, and *The Avengers* came, were seen and conquered the opposition and were *never* out of the Top Ten viewing charts.

But what made *The Avengers* so different? What special ingredient set it aside from its contemporaries? Why was it so popular?

Well, for sheer unabashed style there has never been another programme quite like it. It had that special something that kept viewers glued to their sets week after week, year after year until now, over two decades later, it continues to attract huge viewing figures worldwide and has notched a niche for itself in television history. So, what was that special 'something'? In a word, class.

Consider the facts. The programme was produced by a trio of highly professional film makers (Julian Wintle, Albert Fennell, Brian Clemens); scripted by the finest writing talent of the period (Roger Marshall, Philip Levene, Brian Clemens, Tony Williamson, Terry Nation *et al*) and always attained the highest production values of any television series of the time. Further (and possibly most important of all), every single one of the production staff cared for their product and impregnated the series with that affection – and it showed.

It also had two of the most appealing characters ever to grace the television screen. John Steed, played throughout with conviction and flair by Patrick Macnee, and, well, you pays your money and you takes your choice from the bevy of beautiful and talented ladies who graced his arm. Personally, I've always had a soft spot for Steed's first female assistant, Mrs Catherine Gale (Honor Blackman), yet who could dismiss the alluring Mrs Peel (Diana Rigg); the soft and feminine Miss King (Linda Thorson) or arguably the best *Avengers* girl, Purdey (Joanna Lumley) – each with their own special charm and appeal, and each bringing something special to their portrayal of Steed's Girl Friday.

True, the scripts were occasionally corny and the violence moulded from china clay instead of concrete, but the 'corn' was of the easily digestible variety and the 'violence' played for pantomimic effect. The programme never entered the realms of the absurd and while other programmes of the period echoed the everyday values and conflicts of our work-a-day existence, *The Avengers* begged us to enter its own surrealistic Peter Pan never-never-land – a place where anything could (and often did) happen. It was (and is) escapist fun. Something that gives us the opportunity to leave behind the toils of our work-dominated society and enter a different dimension – a fantasy world. A world peopled by larger-than-life characters. A world in which the whole proceedings are taken with tongue firmly in cheek. That's all it is, fantasy, but produced with flair, style and CLASS.

How it all began – a fascinating shot from the very first* Avengers *story* Hot Snow. *The picture shows Dr David Keel (Ian Hendry) and his fiancée Peggy (Catherine Woodville) on the trail of the heroin package mistakenly delivered to Keel's surgery. This error would cost Peggy her life and propel Dr Keel into an unending crusade to avenge her death.

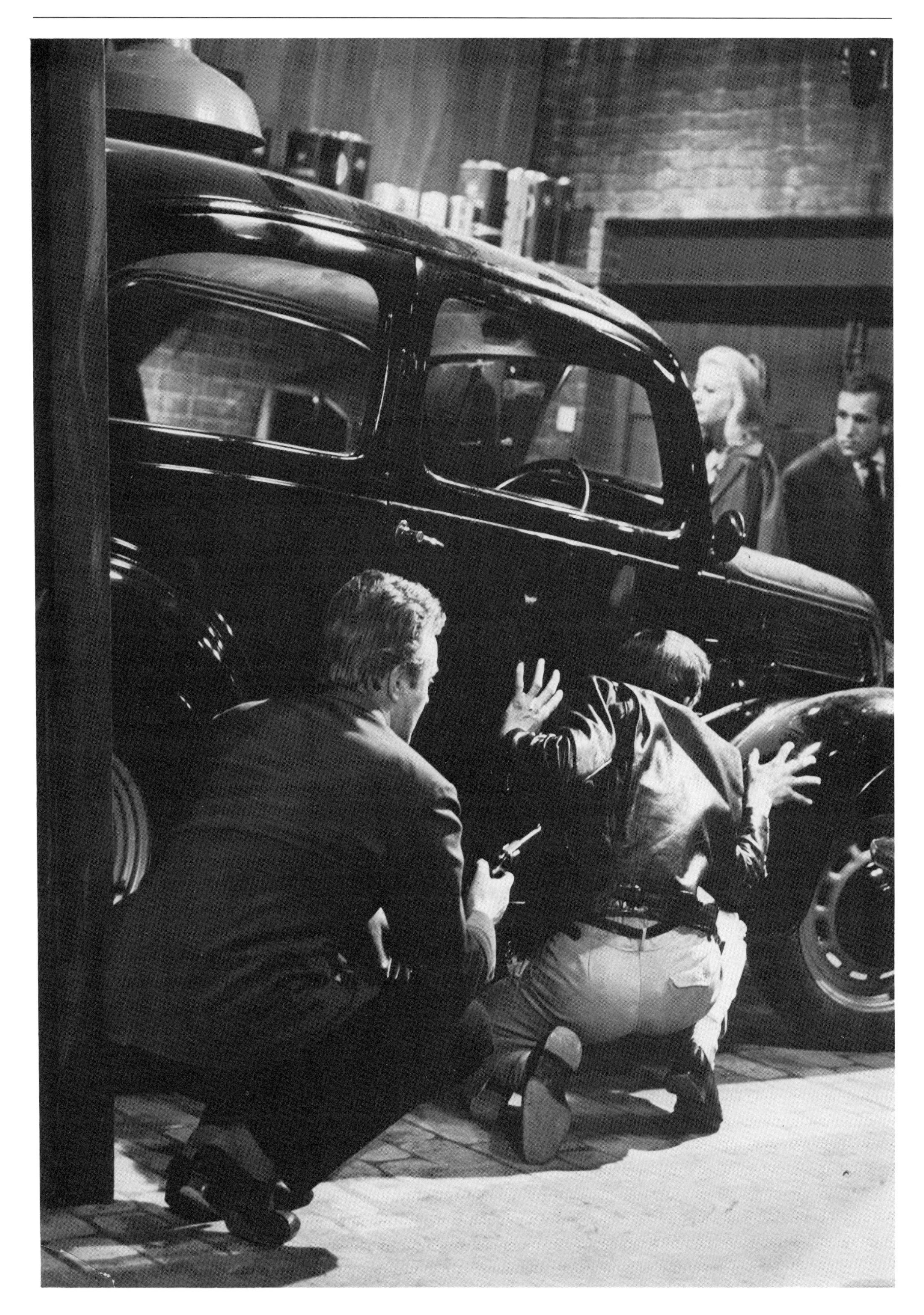

INCREDIBLE STATISTICS

Long before the big screen super-spy boom introduced us to James Bond, that small-screen hero extraordinaire John Steed of *The Avengers* was a household name. The *Avengers* story is an astonishing one. Here are some of its incredible statistics:

☐ It achieved an all-time record of being sold to over 104 countries.

☐ It was the only British series to have achieved the distinction of being networked at prime time in the United States.

☐ Over 187 episodes were produced (161 *Avengers* and 26 *New Avengers*).

☐ 650 miles of film were shot (enough to cover all the villains in the world from end to end).

☐ The series' total running time was 158 hours (enough for flying around the world 3½ times).

☐ Patrick Macnee wore over 40 bowler hats and toted over 30 brollies.

☐ He and his leading ladies imbibed over 20 gallons of champagne.

☐ The *Avengers* girls delivered over 200 karate or kung fu chops.

☐ Over 340 original designs were fashioned and worn.

☐ The cast delivered over 700,000 words of dialogue.

In Spain, the series was known as *Los Vengadores* and was awarded Los Quijotes de Oro by the Spanish Television Critics Society. In Germany they called it *Mit Schirm, Charme und Melone (With Umbrella, Charm and Bowler).* France dubbed it *Le Chapeon Melon et Bottes De Cuir* (*The Bowler Hat and Leather Boots*) and the Macnee/Thorson partnership was awarded Le Prix Triomphe in 1970. In the USA, nineteen years after the show was first transmitted, the series can still be regularly seen (with some stations transmitting two episodes a night, while others screen one episode a night over an 84-day period!) and Diana Rigg was nominated for an Emmy (the TV equivalent of an Oscar).

Whatever title is attached to the show, *The Avengers* is, without question, one of the most popular television series ever produced and has etched its name indelibly into television history.

Emma listens intently in a scene from The Joker.

A THREE-HANDED GAME

The New Avengers

'AVENGING IS EVEN BETTER THAN BEFORE' boasted the *Daily Mail* headline. Shaun Usher, the *Mail's* TV critic, reviewing the episode *The Eagle's Nest*, added: 'Pay no heed to that title. *The New Avengers* are, thank goodness, the old *Avengers*, in fact the very old ones in their Sixties heyday before the show declined in a noticeably wan and shabby final season.' Other critics echoed this view: 'The New Avengers are in sparkling super-active form' *(Sunday Mirror)*; 'It's far-fetched – but great entertainment' *(News of the World)*; 'It's Wham! Bam! Pow stuff!' *(Daily Mirror)*

So, was Avenging really *better* than before? Any attempt to answer that question obviously invites a comparison between the 'new' characters and their highly successful predecessors – three beautiful and talented actresses who, during their time in the series (and depending on one's personal viewpoint, of course), were each regarded as being *the* superlative *Avengers* girl. Certainly all three would prove a hard act to follow.

High praise, then, to Joanna Lumley, who not only accepted the challenge but soon proved that she was a more than worthy successor for the highly coveted role of Steed's new female colleague. She had been described in pre-publicity handouts as: 'Purdey, a girl for the Eighties. A girl who packs ultra-femininity with a fighting style that is effective as it is unique. A girl who can shoot the pips out of an apple at twenty paces. A stockings and suspenders girl – giving lots of glimpses of thigh. A man's woman – a male chauvinist pig's dream.' It is not too surprising that male viewers waited with baited breath (and eager anticipation) for their first glimpse of Steed's new Girl Friday.

Reality, however, isn't always that simple or – in the case of television hype – is seldom what we've been led to believe. Although it soon became obvious to the more discerning viewer that Miss Lumley was indeed wearing 'single-hose', regular views of stocking tops and suspender tabs were all too conspicuous by their absence – with only the rooftop-climbing scenes in *Target* and the titillating close-up of Purdey's black stocking tops in *To Catch a Rat* allowing the onlooker a clear (though all too brief) glimpse of thigh. Mind you, in fairness to Joanna Lumley she did go on record as saying 'I resent being sold as sexy. I'm certainly not a sex symbol, so anyone who expects to find something kinky will be disappointed.'

The much-lauded Purdey 'fighting style' (described as 'Panache', a technique based on the French martial art of self-defence) soon became an added highlight of each episode, with the beautiful and athletic actress delivering shoulder-high kicks and straight right blows to a succession of hapless opponents.

In short, there is little doubt that Joanna Lumley's portrayal of Purdey ranks high on my list of favourite *Avengers* girls and was an inspired piece of casting by producers Albert Fennell and Brian Clemens.

'Mike Gambit, or so rumour has it, was a major in the Paras., and served as a mercenary in the Congo. A man who has clawed his way up through courage, determination and ability. He can be quiet and deceptively still – until he flares into action, when he can strike as fast as a cobra.'

This was how the media introduced the second newcomer, Gareth Hunt, to the series, and like many other *Avengers* loyalists the announcement left me with a feeling of unease. How, I wondered, would this association affect what had previously been seen as a winning format? Indeed, why change the format at all? I had reservations that the introduction of a third member to the team (particularly that of a male) would relegate Steed's character to that of a 'Mother' figure – a kind of 'Mr Waverley' to Gambit and Purdey's 'Solo and Kuryakin' – and leave Steed delegating the action to his younger protégés. Although the first few stories did indeed follow this line, thankfully the situation was soon remedied and Patrick Macnee was once again given a fair percentage of the action. However, the inclusion of Gambit did, as expected, occasionally 'stretch' the storyline at the expense of the action.

As to Gareth Hunt himself. A fine actor, he handled the role of Gambit with complete conviction and his Patrick (Danger Man) McGoohan-style of 'clipped' dialogue added an extra dimension to an otherwise stock television character. His handling of Gambit's action scenes were among the best – if not the best – of any series of *The Avengers*, new or old.

And so to 'Avenger-in-Chief' Patrick Macnee's resumption of the role of John Steed. What can one say about someone who has been the kingpin of *The Avengers* throughout its twenty-odd years' lifespan?

Certainly, considering that Patrick Macnee was forty-seven when the original *Avengers* series ceased production in 1969 and a seven-year gap separated the new series from its predecessor, it is hardly surprising that *Sunday Mirror* columnist Pat Boxhall posed the following question in the issue dated 11 January 1976: 'Can Steed make it again?', then went on to say that as a one-time *Avengers* fan she was alarmed that Patrick Macnee (at fifty-three, and having seen off three glamorous sidekicks) was still being asked to play the sophisticated Steed. She added that he was 'pushing his luck to put a fourth on his arm and did someone in those ivory television towers believe that time doesn't tick-tock for men?' Considering the facts, an understandable question.

Surprisingly, however, it appeared that time had indeed stood still for the ever ebullient Mr Macnee, and though the media led us to believe that 'Steed has mellowed and has now retreated to a large country mansion (Steed's Stud) where he spends most of his time breeding horses and entertaining beautiful women', Steed had, in fact, hardly changed at all.

True, he was slightly heavier – though only in the first few stories; by the time the second thirteen stories began production, Patrick Macnee had slimmed down and looked every bit as suave as the 'slimline' Thorson series model. True, the much-loved Bentley and Rolls-Royce trademarks were no longer in evidence, though a 'reference' to the Bentley did appear in the episode entitled *K is for Kill* – the vehicle seen was rented for one day's shooting, and the Bentley seen in the background as Steed telephones Mrs Peel was courtesy of some unused Rigg colour series film stock. Steed now drove a wide-wheeled, highly polished olive-green Jaguar racing coupé or a choice of two (more practical) Range Rovers. Nevertheless Steed's character hadn't changed.

He still believed in honour and duty. He still retained his olde worlde charm. He still sported his world-famous brolly and bowler – and still looked as immaculate as ever. In short, Patrick Macnee was back as Steed. Avenging, though it was certainly not better than before, was nevertheless well worth waiting for. I have no reservation in urging anyone who missed the series first time around to keep your eyes peeled for any repeat transmission date – you won't be disappointed.

The following twenty-six *New Avengers* episode synopses are listed in the general UK order of transmission and please note that this should not be taken as the chronological order of production.

On the face of it Gambit has become a down-and-out lush, but his appearance is intended to deceive the deceivers in Faces.

THE EAGLE'S NEST

by Brian Clemens

John Steed	**Patrick Macnee**
Mike Gambit	**Gareth Hunt**
Purdey	**Joanna Lumley**
Von Claus	**Peter Cushing**
Father Trasker	**Derek Farr**
Karl	**Frank Gatliff**
Hara	**Sydney Bromley**
Brown-Fitch	**Trevor Baxter**
Lady with dog	**Joyce Carey**
Main	**Neil Phillips**
Stannard	**Brian Anthony**
Barker	**Jerold Wells**
Gerda	**Trude van Dorne**
Nazi Corporal	**Peter Porteous**
Ralph	**Jerold Wells**

Directed by Desmond Davis

PURSUED by fishermen who use rod and line like whips – their hooks dipped in deadly poison – agent Stannard falls to his death, and when his body is later washed ashore, The New Avengers spring into action. Purdey and Steed follow Stannard's trail, while Gambit is delegated to stand in for the dead agent at a lecture being given by Von Claus, an eminent specialist in suspended animation. When Von Claus is abducted, Gambit is forced to fight and win against a young tough named Ralph. Before he can question his prisoner, the youth swallows a suicide capsule and Gambit is left holding one clue – a toupée that covered Ralph's tonsure. Claus meanwhile is taken to the lonely island of St Dorca, a retreat for monks (in reality Nazis intent on forming a new Third Reich). There, he is asked to attend one of the 'brothers' by Father Trasker, their benevolent leader. The treatment proves successful, and Von Claus retires for the evening. As he does so, Brother Karl enters the patient's room and switches off the man's life support system.

Gambit uncovers a link to the island – a plane that crashed there during its flight in 1945 carrying 'Germany's greatest treasure' onboard. Purdey discovers the wreckage, and she and Steed infiltrate the island. They are soon discovered and locked in cells below the monastery. Claus is now informed by Karl that his patient has suffered a relapse and they hurry to the man's side. However, becoming suspicious that the body isn't the same one he attended previously, Claus orders Karl to raise the sheet covering the patient's face. His suspicions are confirmed when the features of Adolf Hitler are revealed and Claus immediately protests his abhorrence at further treatment. However, when Karl informs him that his family are under arrest and wil be killed unless he continues to attend the comatose figure, Claus sees no avenue of escape and prepares to administer the final life-giving injection into the Führer's body. Enter Purdey and Steed who, having engineered their escape, are in turn held at gunpoint by Father Trasker.

At that moment, Gambit breaks into the room and shoots Trasker. As he does so, the man's finger tightens on the machine-gun's trigger and the room is sprayed with stray bullets. Several enter the comatose body, effectively putting an end to Trasker's plans of a new Reich. Exit The New Avengers to the tune of 'The Colonel Bogey March'.

HOUSE OF CARDS

by Brian Clemens

John Steed	**Patrick Macnee**
Mike Gambit	**Gareth Hunt**
Purdey	**Joanna Lumley**
Perov	**Peter Jeffrey**
Roland	**Frank Thornton**
Cartney	**Lyndon Brook**
The Bishop	**Derek Francis**
Spence	**Mark Burns**
Jo	**Geraldine Moffatt**
Suzy	**Annette Andre**
Olga	**Ina Skriver**
David	**Murray Brown**
Vasil	**Gordon Sterne**
Boris	**Dan Meaden**
Tulliver	**Jeremy Wilkin**
Frederick	**Anthony Bailey**

Directed by Ray Austin

A RUSSIAN defector, Professor Vasil, is about to be returned to his homeland at gunpoint by fellow countryman and master-spy Perov. There is a sudden burst of confusion when a group of screaming pop fans, led by Purdey, stampede through the airport lounge in pursuit of their idol – Mike Gambit, masquerading as a pop star. During this confusion, Vasil is led to safety by John Steed. Because of this fiasco, Vasil is ordered home to face the Commissariat. Instead he feigns his death, and after his 'funeral' goes into hiding and sets operation House of Cards into action. The House of Cards is a code system designed by Perov in which Russian 'sleepers', infiltrated into the country during the last twenty years, are sent half-playing cards on receipt of which they become mindless killers, each with a designated target. The King of Hearts is the code to kill Steed; Gambit's name is on the Knave; and Purdey is in line to become the assassinated Queen.

Soon afterwards, close 'friends' of the trio begin to act strangely; Gambit is faced with a fight for his life during a 'friendly' karate session; Purdey saves Steed's life at the hands of his girlfriend; and further assassination attempts are thwarted. Their success, however, is not Perov's ultimate aim – this is to get Steed worried enough for Vasil's safety to race for his secret location and unwittingly lead Perov to the man responsible for his disgrace. Unaware that his car is being shadowed by Perov in a helicopter, Steed does just that and as he is preparing to move Vasil to a new safehouse the men find themselves under fire from Perov. Perov then threatens to kill both men by tossing a grenade into the cottage unless Steed sends out Vasil alone. Steed takes a desperate gamble and, wearing Vasil's clothes, steps through the doorway. He is immediately downed by a shot from Perov's pistol.

Enter Purdey by road and Gambit by air, piloting the Russian's vacated helicopter. Several low-flying swoops send Perov racing into Purdeys waiting arms but, anticipating an easy fight against a woman, the Russian viciously knocks Purdey to the ground. In total disbelief, she springs to her feet and sends Perov sprawling backwards with a right uppercut to the jaw, and as Gambit races to her side the girl exclaims indignantly: 'He *hit* me!'

Purdey and Steed find killing is habit-forming for a group of neo-Nazis at their St Dorca retreat in The Eagle's Nest.

Gambit races from a helicopter to end Perov's attempt to extend his chain of murders in House of Cards.

THE LAST OF THE CYBERNAUTS . . . ?

by Brian Clemens

John Steed	**Patrick Macnee**
Mike Gambit	**Gareth Hunt**
Purdey	**Joanna Lumley**
Kane	**Robert Lang**
Malov	**Oscar Quitak**
Dr Marlow	**Gwen Taylor**
Professor Mason	**Basil Hopkins**
Goff	**Robert Gillespie**
Fitzroy	**David Horovitch**
Laura	**Sally Bazely**
Mrs Weir	**Pearl Hackney**
Second guard	**Martin Fisk**
Terry	**Eric Carte**
First guard	**Ray Armstrong**
Cybernaut	**Rocky Taylor**
Tricia	**Davina Taylor**

Directed by Sidney Hayers

JOHN Steed and Emma Peel had met them before – the Cybernauts. It was over ten years ago and they had nearly died. Steed had forgotten the incident, but when a man named Frank Goff – a man who helped Professor Armstrong construct the deadly robots many years ago – walks free from prison, Steed is once again embroiled in the unfinished business of The Cybernauts.

Months ago, The New Avengers were on the trail of double agent Felix Kane when, during a frantic car chase, Kane's car had collided with a petrol tanker and burst into flames. Steed and his colleagues believed the man had died in the inferno, but Kanes's will to survive was as massive and intense as the flames from which he was dragged. Now, confined to a wheelchair, with his horribly scarred face hidden behind masks, the evil, bland, smiling Kane is determined to accomplish his sole vendetta – the extinction of the New Avengers. Accompanied by Malov, his faithful retainer, Kane abducts Goff and he is forced at gunpoint to reactivate the Cybernauts that are found hidden in a cellar. One of the robots is then sent on a mission of death and destruction until it finally meets its own end at the hands of Gambit and Purdey.

Undaunted, Kane sends a second Cybernaut to abduct Professor Mason, a leading cybernetics expert. Mason is then forced to formulate a system of cybernetic limbs whereby Kane – his brain linked by electronic pulses to the Cybernaut's power – becomes half-man, half machine. Armed with his newly-found killing power and his burning hatred for the New Avengers, Kane then sets out to dispose of his immediate target – Purdey – his intention being to mutilate her body to such a degree that it will cause Steed mental anguish until he, too, meets death at Kane's powerful hands. Gambit, waiting for his colleague outside her flat, is unable to prevent Kane's advance and finds himself hurtled to the ground by a single blow from Kane's fist. Kane now turns his attention to Purdey's door and within seconds the door is smashed apart. Purdey is now faced with the fight of her life, and the two are soon embroiled in deadly combat. Enter Steed who, handing Gambit an aerosol spray, races to Purdey's defence. The can's contents are sprayed on to Kane's body and soon his flailing arms shudder to a halt until, finally, the monstrous figure becomes immobile. Kane's eyes burn with intense anger as he is shown the can's label, 'PLASTIC SKIN - good for 1,001 uses', and Steed utters the words: 'A thousand and *two.*'

The lethal cybernaut goes into action against Gambit. Seconds after this encounter, Gambit's fists cause the cybernaut to lose its head.

THE MIDAS TOUCH

by Brian Clemens

John Steed	**Patrick Macnee**
Mike Gambit	**Gareth Hunt**
Purdey	**Joanna Lumley**
Freddy	**John Carson**
Vann	**Ed Devereaux**
Hong Kong Harry	**Ronald Lacey**
Turner	**David Swift**
Lieutenant	**Jeremy Child**
Curator	**Robert Mill**
Garvin	**Ray Edwards**
Midas	**Gilles Millinaire**
Sing	**Pik-Sen Lim**
Doctor	**Chris Tranchell**
Tayman	**Lionel Guyett**
Simpson	**Geoffrey Bateman**

Directed by Robert Fuest

THE New Avengers are on hand to meet the arrival of 'The Fat Man's' plane. The man turns out to be 'Hong Kong' Harry, an old adversary of Steed's, but he is so fat that Steed fails to recognise him until Harry is downed by a sniper's bullet. Steed and his colleagues are astonished to see a flow of gold dust run from the wound in Harry's ample stomach. Harry's 'belly', they discover, contains over £750,000 worth of gold dust – all neatly packed in small sacks. This discovery leads the trio, together with Freddy, an ex-colleague of Steed's now down on his luck, to the deadly secret of Professor Turner, a man with a lust for gold. Turner, they later discover, has rendered Midas – an Adonis of a young man with a smooth and blandly youthful face – a carrier of every disease known to man. Although Midas himself remains immune, his merest touch on the naked skin spells death to any living thing. Harry's gold dust was meant as part-payment to be given to Turner at an auction of Midas' powers. The auction goes ahead as planned and, to demonstrate Midas' killing power, Turner orders the youth to wipe out the entire assemblage of guests. Vann, a foreign diplomat with demagogic ideas, is so impressed at the demonstration that he agrees to exchange a valuable collection of gold antiquities for Midas. The killer will then assassinate a visiting foreign princess, simply by being presented to her at the gold exhibition.

Steed gets a call from Freddy, but before they can meet, his colleague commits suicide after being touched by Midas during an escape attempt. Purdey, acting on her own, discovers a lead to the plot from a commando officer who used to work with Turner. She infiltrates Turner's office, but is overpowered by a guard and taken prisoner ... and promised to Midas upon completion of his mission. Steed and Gambit find a lead to Purdey's abductors when Gambit breaks into a foreign embassy and proves his worth by beating the embassy guard in a karate match. They arrive at the gold exhibition at the very second that Midas is due to be presented to the princess and quickly proceed to mop up Vann and his cohorts while Purdey, heedful of her colleague's warning cry, 'Don't let him touch you', sets about Midas. A well-timed kick sends the death merchant reeling backwards into an empty mummy case and Gambit races over and slams the lid. The trio then turn their attention to Turner, who was accidentally touched by Midas during the fight and now writhes in plague-ridden agony.

***Gambit takes on a temporary guise of a bejewelled rock star abetted by Purdey in a bid to prevent a top scientist being abducted in* House of Cards.**

CAT AMONGST THE PIGEONS

by Dennis Spooner

John Steed	**Patrick Macnee**
Mike Gambit	**Gareth Hunt**
Purdey	**Joanna Lumley**
Zarcardi	**Vladek Sheybal**
Turner	**Matthew Long**
Rydercroft	**Basil Dignam**
Waterflow	**Peter Copley**
Lewington	**Hugh Walters**
Bridlington	**Gordon Rollings**
Hudson	**Joe Black**
Foster	**Patrick Connor**
Tomkins	**Kevin Stoney**
Merton	**Andrew Bradford**
Controller	**Brian Jackson**

Directed by John Hough

AFTER telling Steed that Rydercroft, Controller of the Ministry of Ecology, is due to die at noon that day, Merton's body is found in coma and from the wreckage of his crashed car Purdey plucks a feather. Steed and his colleagues are in attendance as the plane due to take Rydercroft to Switzerland is about to depart. At 11.55 all is well ... 11.56 and the plane is airborne ... 11.58 ... 11.59 ... all is well aloft – visibility 100%, not another thing in the sky. But at noon the plane disappears off the radar screen. Among the fragmented pieces of the plane found scattered across the countryside is a small ring used for 'ringing' birds. On it are printed the words Sanctuary of Wings. Feathers by the hundred are also found, leading Gambit and Purdey to suspect that the plane was hit by a flock of wild birds. They discover that the bird sanctuary is run by a strange little man named Zarcardi, a man who, because of his unpopular ideas concerning bird conservation, has been ostracised by his fellow ecologists – the majority of whom now appear to be falling victim of bird attacks.

While Steed and Gambit visit Professor Waterlow, a man mentioned by the dying Merton, Purdey dons her motorcycle gear and speeds off to the bird sanctuary. Steed and the Professor are soon forced to seek refuge in a swimming pool when they are attacked by hundreds of screeching birds. Later, on leaving the Professor's home, Steed has to ward off a second attempt when a large bird, planted earlier by Zarcardi, tries to attack him during his drive home. The agent seeks refuge in the back of an open removal truck where, under cover of darkness, he traps the bird beneath his bowler. Purdey meanwhile enters a huge room filled with exotic plants and hundreds of species of birds. As she does so, a small bird alights on her hand and begins to chirp merrilly away until Zarcardi, who has arrived back at the sanctuary and been 'informed' of Purdey's presence, proceeds to play a strange, flute-like instrument. The sound of it has an astonishing effect on the small bird, which immediately draws blood. Purdey now finds herself in a locked room, surrounded by hundreds of screeching feathered assassins.

Enter Steed and Gambit who, armed with baskets of the 'enemy' (cats), proceed to pluck the birds' feathers. During his attempted escape, Zarcardi falls to his death, for as the two agents exclaim: 'He could sing ... but he couldn't fly!'

TARGET

by Dennis Spooner

John Steed	**Patrick Macnee**
Mike Gambit	**Gareth Hunt**
Purdey	**Joanna Lumley**
Draker	**Keith Barron**
Ilenko	**Robert Beatty**
Bradshaw	**Roy Boyd**
Jones	**Frederick Jaeger**
Myers	**Malcolm Stoddard**
Kloekoe	**Deep Roy**
Kendrick	**John Paul**
Lopez	**Bruce Purchase**
Talmadge	**Dennis Blanch**
Palmer	**Robert Tayman**

Directed by Ray Austin

WHEN five top agents die of 'natural' causes, Steed, suspecting foul play, asks Dr Kendrick to investigate further. The doctor finds three tiny marks – barely pin-pricks – on the agents' bodies and confirms Steed's suspicions. Someone, it seems, is depleting Steed's department by curare poisoning. Meanwhile, Draker and his midget aide Kloekoe gloat in the shadows. Steed and Gambit recall that all the agents had recently applied for leave and all had taken their practical test – target practice on an intricate shooting range which is in fact a mock-up street, complete with shops and houses and cut-out characters of life-size figures. Each agent has to traverse the target range shooting down 'enemy' figures that suddenly spring up and avoid getting 'hit' himself, in which event a red spot appears on the 'hit' areas of the body. The test is further complicated by 'friendly' figures, and an agent shooting one of these has points deducted from his score. Only one man has ever achieved a 100% score – John Steed, and he did it three times in succession.

Determined to equal her colleague's record, Purdey sets off down the range shooting 'enemy' figures with ease until, on completing the course, she is informed by Bradshaw, the course controller, that she has in fact received one 'hit' and achieved only a 99% score. Disgusted by her performance, Purdey drives home – little knowing that the single 'hit' marks her for death. The course has been sabotaged by Draker and Kloekoe who, in cahoots with Bradshaw, are determined to prove to Ilenko, a compatriot, that they can decimate Steed's deparment personnel at will. Draker has loaded the 'enemy' figure's guns with tiny ampoules of glass dipped into a curare derivative, and once an agent is 'hit' the poison is released, bringing death within hours.

Draker's plans go awry, however, when Gambit plays a joke on Bradshaw – a joke that misfires and sends a spot-ridden Bradshaw reeling into Gambit's arms. Before dying, he whispers the words: 'Hat ... Steed's hat ... antidote', words that confirm Gambit's suspicions and send him and Steed racing to Purdey's side. Matters worsen further when Steed himself falls victim of the drug – injected by Kloekoe during their visit to Purdey's flat – and it is left to Gambit to run the gauntlet of Draker's killing machine and Kloekoe's deadly blowpipe before recovering the antidote and saving his colleagues.

In Target *cardboard cut-outs that can kill force Purdey to take refuge among the rooftops.*

In Cat Amongst the Pigeons, *Zarcardi, in the inner chamber of his Sanctuary of Wings, tells Purdey that his army of birds will control the world.*

TO CATCH A RAT

by Terence Feeley

John Steed	**Patrick Macnee**
Mike Gambit	**Gareth Hunt**
Purdey	**Joanna Lumley**
Gunner	**Ian Hendry**
Cromwell	**Edward Judd**
Quaintance	**Robert Fleming**
Cledge	**Barry Jackson**
Grant	**Anthony Sharp**
Finder	**Jeremy Hawk**
Operator	**Bernice Stegers**
Nurse	**Jo Kendall**
Farmer	**Dallas Cavell**
Mother	**Sally-Jane Spencer**

Directed by James Hill

SEVENTEEN years ago, Irwin Gunner, an agent operating in the Eastern sector, came within an ace of exposing the identity of 'The White Rat' – a double agent who had betrayed his colleagues. But all Gunner had managed to do was to fire a bullet into his quarry's leg before the traitor got away, unidentified. Gunner's cover had been that of a trapeze artist. He was the 'flyer' and his partner Cledge, also an agent, the 'catcher'. Cledge, however, was in the White Rat's pay, and during a big top performance he had failed to catch his 'flyer' and Gunner fell to the saw dust below. For seventeen years he had lived with a loss of memory. Now, as the result of a knock on the head during a children's game, Gunner's memory is unfrozen and he immediately begins to transmit a message, 'The flyer has landed', to Steed's department – a message that, though transmitted in obsolete code, is urgent enough to have Steed send Gambit and Purdey racing across the countryside to locate its source. Unknown to Steed, the message had also been overheard by Cledge and the traitor who, reasoning that it can only be Gunner, decide he must die before exposing their secret. Cledge discovers their quarry, but Gunner kills him before transmitting a further message that he will 'cut off the Rat's tail'.

Later, when Purdey breaks into Cledge's flat, she discovers Cromwell, head of deparment DIC, rifling through Cledge's belongings. The man gets amorous, and Purdey is forced to cool his ardour by offering to repair his torn trouser leg. Meanwhile, Steed and Gambit decide to lay a trap for the traitor. They suspect Quaintance, a ministry official who walks with a pronounced limp, but when questioned, the man reveals that he received the injury while 'going over the wall'. Pressed further, he reveals that his replacement in the Eastern sector had been shot in the leg – by whom or why was never made clear. The replacement's name, they discover, is Cromwell. Purdey, meanwhile, is avoiding further advances from Cromwell who, having expressed interest in her colleague's plan to net the traitor, receives a phone call from Gunner and the couple race to his location. Fortunately, Gunner becomes impatient at their late arrival and rings a second time. The call is taken by Gambit and he and Steed race after their colleague. They arrive too late, and enter as Gunner, dying from Cromwell's gunshot wound, recovers consciousness long enough to complete his mission with a shot to Cromwell's heart – a shot that was fired seventeen years late.

***Purdey prepares to chase at high speed through the countryside trying to track down 'The Flyer' who is sending messages over government airwaves in* To Catch a Rat.**

TALE OF THE BIG WHY

by Brian Clemens

John Steed	**Patrick Macnee**
Mike Gambit	**Gareth Hunt**
Purdey	**Joanna Lumley**
Harmer	**Derek Waring**
Irene	**Jenny Runacre**
Brandon	**George Cooper**
Turner	**Roy Marsden**
Roach	**Gary Waldhorn**
Poole	**Rowland Davis**
Minister	**Geoffrey Toone**
Mrs Turner	**Maeve Alexander**

Directed by Robert Fuest

BERT Brandon had been trying to do a deal with the government for years. His information, he told them, would rock Whitehall to its foundations but they wouldn't bite and now, as Brandon leaves prison, he is determined to recover the document he had hidden and sell it to the highest bidder. The day he walks through the prison gates, four people are waiting: Poole and Roach – two foreign 'heavies' – Purdey and Gambit. Within hours, Brandon dies – hurled backwards into the rear seat of his car by the shots from Poole and Roach's automatics. The ensuing chase ends with Purdey being thrown headlong from her motorcycle into a rock a few feet away from the remains of Brandon's car – demolished by the two hoodlums during their unsuccessful search for Brandon's secret. Gambit races to Purdey's rescue and they remove Brandon's boots from the wreckage – boots that when X-rayed show traces of Diolyhyde, a chemical used in crop spraying. The clue leads them to Turner, a friend of Brandon's who supplements his earning by crop-dusting. Turner, however, soon finds himself on the run and is chased by Poole and Roach,who are in turn pursued by Purdey and Gambit as they race to Turner's rescue. After the chase, Purdey is told by Turner's wife that Brandon visited the farm and left a package to be posted to his daughter, Irene. Steed visits the girl and she willingly hands him the package, but to his surprise it contains only a western paperback book called, *The Tale of the Big Why.* The book obviously holds a clue – but to what?

After much deliberation, the trio crack the code and realise that the 'tale' is in fact the *'tail'* of the letter Y in Surrey, as denoted on an aviator's map of the county. However, their efforts to locate Brandon's secret are thwarted by Irene Brandon who, in cahoots with Turner, has reached the same conclusion. The trio stay one jump ahead, and are soon involved in a cross-country chase that eventually leads to Purdey being abducted by Poole and Roach who, having demanded the document in exchange for the girl, meet with a 'laughter-filled' end; Gambit playing a 'dangerous game' with Turner's plane; and Steed playing a deadly game of chess with Home Office official, Harmer, before exposing him as the traitor named in Brandon's document.

Steed, Harmer and the government minister discuss the release of a prisoner who claims he has secrets which could shake the government to its foundations – a scene from **Tale of the Big Why.**

In Faces, *Purdey, in the guise of a Salvationist, speaks faith to an old sundowner in the Mission for the Distressed and Needy.*

Purdey becomes 'Today's Biggest Offer' in a window display to evade her armed pursuers in Sleeper.

FACES

by Brian Clemens and Dennis Spooner

John Steed	**Patrick Macnee**
Mike Gambit	**Gareth Hunt**
Purdey	**Joanna Lumley**
Prator	**David De Keyser**
Mullins	**Edward Petherbridge**
Clifford	**Neil Hallett**
Wendy	**Annabel Leventon**
Bilston	**David Webb**
Sheila	**Jill Melford**
Craig	**Richard Leech**
Torrance	**Donald Hewlett**
Attendant	**Robert Putt**
Tramp	**J.G. Devlin**
Peters	**Michael Sheard**

Directed by James Hill

SPOTTING the similarity between himself and Home Office official Craig, Terrison, a drifter, and his cohort Mullins kill the man and Terrison replaces him. They join forces with Dr Prator, a brilliant plastic surgeon, and begin to recruit down-and-outs from the Mission for the Distressed and Needy and use them to replace high-ranking government officials. The down-and-outs' faces must be similar to someone in the government and they are then brainwashed and sent to replace the victims. Craig's plans, however are soon threatened with exposure when their latest 'double' – a lookalike for Mark Clifford, a close friend of Steed's – dies within days of replacing the man, an event that brings Steed into the picture. Convinced that the Mission holds a clue, Steed delegates Mike Gambit to pose as an unkempt alcoholic and infiltrate the place. Gambit does so, and is soon spotted as an ideal replacement for 'Gambit'. Purdey, acting independently, visits the Mission disguised as a prim Salvation Army official and, finding a link with Craig, she returns masquerading as 'Lolita', a cheap and dowdy tart. Craig meanwhile orders Prator to find a 'double' for John Steed – an opportunity that swiftly arrives when a Steed 'lookalike' is found in a drunken stupor.

Informed by 'Lolita' that she is wanted by the police, Prator, aware that 'with some work' the girl could pass for Purdey, agrees to help her and she is taken to meet 'Mike Gambit'. Gambit, however, fails to recognise his colleague and, believing that Prator has discovered a replacement for Purdey, telephones Steed and tells him that Purdey's life may be in danger. Craig now orders Prator to advance the 'treatment' on their Steed 'lookalike', and later, satisfied that the 'double' is ready, he drives the man to Steed's country home, hands him a gun and orders him to dispose of Steed. A shot through an open window achieves that end, and the men drive away smiling.

It now becomes a case of who can Purdey trust? Is it *really* 'Purdey'. Is Steed really *Steed?* Which Gambit *is* Gambit? Matters are soon resolved when Steed exposes Craig, and Gambit, suspected by Purdey of being a double, saves face by throwing a well-timed punch to Craig's jaw as he holds Steed at gunpoint ... proving beyond doubt that, though 'two-faced', there is only *one* Mike Gambit!

SLEEPER

by Brian Clemens

John Steed	**Patrick Macnee**
Mike Gambit	**Gareth Hunt**
Purdey	**Joanna Lumley**
Brady	**Keith Buckley**
Tina	**Sara Kestelman**
Chuck	**Mark Jones**
Bart	**Prentis Hancock**
Bill	**Leo Dolan**
Ben	**Dave Schofield**
Fred	**Gavin Campbell**
Carter	**Peter Godfrey**
Hardy	**Joe Dunne**
Policemen	**Jason White**
	Rony McHale
Dr Graham	**Arthur Dignam**

Directed by Graeme Clifford

THE New Avengers are told by Hardy, one of Steed's field agents, that something 'big' is about to happen connected with S.95, a new anti-terrorist weapon – a colourless, odourless gas which can put a man to sleep for a minimum of six hours unless he has been injected with the antidote – so they attend a demonstration of the gas. However, all seems to run smoothly and they leave. As they depart, Brady – previously disguised as Professor Marco, the inventor of S.95 – overpowers a guard and steals several canisters of the gas together with a supply of antidote capsules. Steed, spending the night at Gambit's apartment, is concerned when he unsuccessfully tries to renew contact with Hardy. His worries increase further when, during the early hours of the following morning, his colleague's 'pet' sparrow Charlie is found fast asleep on Gambit's window ledge. Suspecting a link with Hardy's message, Steed telephones Purdy and asks her to check the area outside her flat. Meanwhile, a helicopter flies low over the city releasing vast quantities of S.95 over a designated area and in the streets below, unhindered by the sleeping populace, Brady and his gang begin their joyride – looting major banking houses as they tour the deserted streets.

Purdey finds the neighbourhood full of sleeping figures and, returning to her flat, tries to relay her findings to her colleagues. Her attempt to do so is hampered by finding her flat door securely closed, and further contact is made impossible when Brady's men sever the telephone wires to the area. Now alone and dressed only in her slippers and pyjama suit, Purdey decides to drive to Gambit's apartment. Her colleagues reach a similar decision, and unwittingly pass her on her drive across town.

The scenario is now set for a cross-city chase between the trio and Brady's gang of cut-throats. A chase that is fraught with danger for the agents who, unarmed, are forced to ward off numerous attacks by Brady's armed cohorts. Dropping heavies as she goes, Purdey finally reaches the river. However, though the opposite side beckons safety, she is unable to find a crossing point and she continues her search. Meanwhile, her colleagues have reached 'high ground' (the Post Office Tower) and, spotting the gang's departure point, they soon overpower them. Then, dressed in their captives' clothing they make their way to a waiting helicopter – only to find Purdey asleep at the controls. Within minutes, they too fall fast asleep.

THE THREE-HANDED GAME

by Dennis Spooner and Brian Clemens

John Steed	**Patrick Macnee**
Mike Gambit	**Gareth Hunt**
Purdey	**Joanna Lumley**
Ranson	**David Wood**
Juventor	**David Greif**
Ivan	**Tony Vogel**
Larry	**Michael Petrovitch**
Professoe Meroff	**Terry Wood**
Masgard	**Gary Raymond**
Tony Field	**Noel Trevarthen**

Directed by Ray Austin

MASTER spy Juventor and his aide Ivan have stolen a sophisticated apparatus that transfers the thoughts and physical skills from one person to another by 'scrambling' their brain – leaving the donors' bodies mindless vegetables. Their first victim is 'Taps' Ranson, a professional dancer, and Juventor then arranges a demonstration of the machine for Colonel Meroff, a foreign ambassador, in which Ranson's psyche is transferred into Meroff's body. Flushed with the machine's possibilities, Meroff offers Juventor ten million pounds to obtain details of 'The Three-Handed Game' – a top secret 4,000-word document which, designed by Steed, has been 'entrusted' to three agents, Masgard, McKay and Fields, each of whom has a photographic memory and, like a computer, can 'bank' endless information until called on to reveal it at a later date. Each agent has received one-third of the code – parts which, without the others, are useless.

Steed gets an idea of Juventor's plans from Larry, one of his field agents who, though succumbing to Juventor's machine, manages to reach Steed before being hospitalised. Juventor, however, is convinced that The New Avengers are on his trail, and permanently transfers his own psyche into Ranson's body before setting off to obtain the secrets from the agents. When 'Juventor's' body is found, Steed is suspicious of the ploy and delegates himself to guard Fields; Gambit is ordered to McKay; and Purdey is given the task of protecting Masgard. Masgard, a professional memory-man, is the first to receive the 'treatment' and his brain is scrambled after an evening performance, while Purdey 'clowns' about in the next room. Steed, too, is unable to prevent racing-driver Fields from imparting his third of the code, and Steed immediately doubles the guard on McKay, a young female artist. However, even the combined forces of Purdey and Gambit prove insufficient to halt Juventor's plans, and McKay's secret is soon added to Juventor's shopping list. In receipt of the complete code, the spy now rings Meroff and demands payment.

Juventor has, of course, reckoned without the combined forces of all three Avengers and, in a deserted theatre setting, he has to face a merry dance from Purdey's shapely legs and feet before she rings down the curtain on his plans.

Steed successfully outstrips Field's Formula One car but fails to put a brake on Juventor's brain machine in **The Three-Handed Game.**

DIRTIER BY THE DOZEN

by Brian Clemens

John Steed	Patrick Macnee
Mike Gambit	Gareth Hunt
Purdey	Joanna Lumley
Colonel Miller	John Castle
Sergeant Bowden	Shaun Curry
Travis	Colin Skeaping
General Stevens	Michael Barrington
Captain Tony Noble	Michael Howarth
Terry	Brian Croucher

Directed by Sidney Hayers

GENERAL Stevens, arriving at Colonel 'Mad Jack' Miller's special 19th Commando Unit for a 'spot check', finds the place deserted but is later killed when Miller and his unit arrive back from a mysterious jungle campaign. The General's disappearance brings Steed, Gambit and Purdey into action. Gambit receives two reels of film in the post – films that contain scenes of jungle fighting in various parts of the world and, after several viewings, Purdey and Gambit find a common link between the newsreels. Colonel Miller had been filmed everywhere from the war-torn Middle East to the jungles of Latin America; the question is, how could Miller have been fighting in so many wars – especially when he is a serving British officer?

Miller's army record shows that his unit is made up from the dregs of army personnel – the rogues and malingerers – from which such unpromising material Miller has forged a formidable fighting unit. Steed suspects the unit is being hired out as mercenaries – Miller's own private army, in fact. Further investigations are called for, so Steed delegates Gambit to join the unit. Purdey visits Miller's base alone and, after questioning his men, is arrested by Miller and accused of being a spy. Gambit, posing as a Major, arrives at the base and meets with more success when Miller tells him that his army record – allegations about missing army funds; appropriation of army property, etc – points to Gambit being either a fool or extremely cunning. His record is in fact despicable ... and the best recommendation he could have to join the 19th Commando!

Steed, having checked on the equipment purchased by Miller for his next campaign, discovers that everything points to the Middle East – a place where banks are loaded with money and the mosques laden with gold. He is further concerned that Miller intends to leave the missing General's body on the spot, thus implicating the British Army and instigating the possibility of World War 3. The question now is, can Miller be stopped in time? Before that question can be answered, Gambit engineers Purdey's escape – only to find he has landed her into a minefield from which Steed is forced to extricate both his colleagues and the solution. Miller chooses a 'military' death, and Purdey is given an 'in flight' glass of champagne – courtesy of John Steed.

In Dirtier by the Dozen, *Purdey seeks information from her uncle, Colonel Elroyd Foster, about the disappearance of General Stevens, and gleans some disturbing facts.*

GNAWS

by Dennis Spooner

John Steed	**Patrick Macnee**
Mike Gambit	**Gareth Hunt**
Purdey	**Joanna Lumley**
Charles Thornton	**Julian Holloway**
Walters	**Morgan Shepherd**
Carter	**Peter Cellier**
Harlow	**John Watts**
Girl	**Anulka Dubinska**
Motor Mechanic	**Ronnie Laughlin**
Ivan Chislenko	**Jeremy Young**
George Ratcliffe	**Patrick Malahide**
Joe	**Keith Marsh**
Arthur	**Ken Wynne**
Malloy	**Keith Alexander**
Couple in car	**Denise Reynolds**
	Peter Richardson

Directed by Ray Austin

TWELVE months earlier Steed and his colleagues had investigated the death of Marlow, an agent who had been on surveillance security duty at the Ministry of Agriculture. At the time there had been little evidence to link the agent's death to a clumsy robbery of secret papers connected with research into the growth of living things through radioactivity. Marlow's death, it appeared, had been coincidence. However, Thornton and his assistant Carter had been responsible for both crimes. Thornton had left six weeks later, but Carter stayed on and together they had entered into business alone. Unhampered by red tape, they had cut corners and taken risks to grow things to enormous proportions. Their experiments were meant to help mankind, but things started to go awry when Carter carelessly split some radioactive isotope and washed it down the sink. Since that day, reports of 'someting nasty in the sewers' had started circulating, and when a gang of maintenance men disappear while checking the sewers The New Avengers are asked to investigate.

Gambit and Purdey discover that rats are few and far between in a place that would normally be teeming with them. They also meet Chislenko, their opposite number, and for once East and West unite against a common foe – whatever is down there, they decide, has grown ravenous and has started to hunt human prey. Meanwhile, alarmed that their mistake will lead to their exposure, Thornton and Carter arm themselves and enter the sewers to destroy their 'creation'. Carter soon falls victim of the unseen 'monster' and his colleague retreats to safety – only to find himself confronted by Chislenko who, believing the man to be responsible for the killings, tries to arrest him. The Russian is shot, and Thornton escapes.

Purdey searches the Ministry records and finds a connection with the previous break-in – a giant tomato! Her two colleagues meanwhile concoct a foul-smelling mixture that they hope will bring the 'monster' into the open, and enter the sewers. Hearing Thornton's shot, Purdey races to the scene and quickly finds herself held at gunpoint by the scientist and in danger of being used as 'live' bait. Racing to her rescue, Gambit puts pay to the beast – an enormous rat – with an armour-piercing rocket gun. Purdey shows her appreciation by serving her colleagues a giant tomato salad – a dish they soon confess is guaranteed to last for not just one meal, but the next ... and the next ... and the next ...

DEAD MEN ARE DANGEROUS

by Brian Clemens

John Steed	**Patrick Macnee**
Mike Gambit	**Gareth Hunt**
Purdey	**Joanna Lumley**
Mark	**Clive Revill**
Perry	**Richard Murdoch**
Penny	**Gabrielle Drake**
Hara	**Terry Taplin**
Dr Culver	**Michael Turner**
Sandy	**Trevor Adams**
Headmaster	**Roger Avon**

Directed by Sidney Hayers

AFTER deciding to round off their evening with a nightcap, Steed and Purdey enter Steed's home to find the place vandalised. The agent's valuable art and porcelain collection lies smashed in the fireplace and later a bomb explodes in Steed's garage – writing off his beloved Bentley. Further events happen in swift succession: a coffin bearing the inscription JOHN STEED – R.I.P. arrives at Steed's home; Gambit finds that Steed's school sporting mementoes have been destroyed; and Steed twice escapes death from a sniper's bullet – or were the shots meant as a warning? Someone, it seems, is intent on destroying all the things Steed cares for, trying to deny his very existence. Finally, Steed's mental anguish is stretched to the breaking point by a message that Purdey has been abducted and will die at 5am that day.

Gambit discovers a clue to the abductor's identity – Mark Crayford, an old school chum and ex-colleague of Steed's who, during an East-West border incident ten years previously, had 'crossed over' to the enemy. Steed had been forced to shoot him, and his bullet had lodged dangerously near to Crayford's heart. During the intervening years, the bullet had moved almost an inch, bringing the man close to death, and now Crayford has returned to wreak vengeance on his 'killer'. A clue to the man's whereabouts is also discovered on a tape-recording made during his Ministry medical. It contains references to 'The Victorian Folly' – a deserted bell tower in the country where, as children, Crayford had achieved his one and only victory over Steed. Purdey meanwhile finds herself chained to a wall of the tower and is forced to listen to Crayford's cravings as he rants on about his final victory over Steed, a victory that will be complete with Purdey's death. The hands on the clock read 4.48 and Purdey's fears increase.

Gambit informs Steed of his discovery and the two men race to the bell tower. As Steed enters, he uses his steel-lined bowler to deflect Crayford's shot. Undaunted, Crayford turns to face his nemesis and beams with delight at having his quarry in his gunsight. However, seconds later, when Gambit bursts into the room he is astonished to find his colleagues safe, and confused to find Crayford lying dead on the floor. Purdey clears up the mystery when she tells hims: 'Steed shot him ... ten years ago.'

***Gambit stalks the monster in the sewers in* Gnaws.**

Steed about to hurl his bowler at Mark Crayford, who is holding Purdey at gunpoint, in Dead Men are Dangerous.

Steed lines up his squad of mini-skirted rock fans who are about to play havoc with one of the world's most cunning foreign agents in House of Cards.

ANGELS OF DEATH

by Terence Feely and Brian Clemens

John Steed	**Patrick Macnee**
Mike Gambit	**Gareth Hunt**
Purdey	**Joanna Lumley**
Manderson	**Terence Alexander**
Tammy	**Caroline Munro**
Reresby	**Michael Latimer**
Pelbright	**Richard Gale**
Jane	**Lindsay Duncan**
Wendy	**Pamela Stephenson**
Cindy	**Colonel Tomson**
Sally Manderson	**Melissa Stribling**
Simon Carter	**Anthony Bailey**

Directed by Ernest Day

STEED and Purdey are on the scene when agent Martin returns to the West by crashing down a lonely border post – only to be gunned down moments later by a sniper's bullet. Before dying, Martin whispers: 'Angel of Death ... the killer within.' Back home, The New Avengers attend a departmental meeting headed by Pelbright, a man who looks fit and well after a week on a health farm. However, immediately after opening a folder with a strange maze doodled upon it, Pelbright shows signs of stress and within minutes dies – from 'natural' causes. Further investigations reveal that forty-seven other agents had died in similar circumstances within the last two years. All had three things in common: each had held secret Ministry posts; all had died within days of each other; and all had died from 'natural' causes. Steed believes that there is a missing fourth factor – one that must be found soon.

Later that day, Steed and Head of Security, Colonel Tomson, are out clay pigeon shooting and the man tells Steed that he never felt better since returning from a week's course at a health farm. Suddenly, however, Thompson falls over dead. Later, when the post mortem points to death from 'natural' causes, Steed reasons that the missing fourth factor could be connected to the health farm and decides to book in for treatment. Purdey, reaching the same conclusion and acting independently, also pays the health clinic a visit. She is discovered while searching a room and soon finds herself strapped to a huge traction machine. Gambit meanwhile is reading the clinic's prospectus and decides that he, too, should investigate further.

Steed's arrival is greeted with elation by the clinic's staff and he soon finds himself the victim of the 'the killer within'. The clinic is being used as a cover for a gigantic brainwashing complex, in which agents under stress are trapped in a maze and, like a rat in a trap which smells food but can't get to it, they eventually go mad – or die – in their attempt. Steed is now trapped in the maze and being given the 'treatment'. Meanwhile Coldstream, a Ministry official responsible for the operation, orders his cohorts to interrogate Purdey. Purdey, however, has been rescued by Gambit and while her colleague mops up Coldstream's gang, she attempts to locate Steed. In the process she, too, finds herself trapped between the advancing maze walls and it is left to Gambit to become an 'Angel of Mercy' and rescue his colleagues in the nick of time.

Steed in a semi-drugged state waits behind a door as Reresby enters with his gun at the ready, in a scene from Angels of Death.

MEDIUM RARE

by Dennis Spooner

John Steed	Patrick Macnee
Mike Gambit	Gareth Hunt
Purdey	Joanna Lumley
Wallace	Jon Finch
Elderly man	Mervyn Johns
Richards	Jeremy Wilkin
Victoria Stanton	Sue Holderness
Roberts	Neil Hallett
McBain	Maurice O'Connell
Dowager lady	Diana Churchill
Model girl	Celia Foxe
Man in seance	Steve Ubels
Mason	Allen Weston

Directed by Ray Austin

THE New Avengers are investigating the sudden death of Steed's friend and colleague, Freddy Mason – a man who had been acting as paymaster to a team of informers. Wallace, Mason's boss, had set up the informers' team and then, by a series of clever and elaborate disguises, had used the operation to line his own pockets. Now Wallace, knowing that Steed will dig and keep on digging until he has discovered his friend's killer, hires Richards, a professional killer, to first frame and then eliminate Steed.

Help comes from an unexpected source – Victoria Stanton, a 'fake' medium who suddenly realises her powers when she 'foresees' Steed's death. Gambit and Purdey refuse to take her warnings seriously, however, until she predicts that Steed will receive a communication from overseas; will unexpectedly have to walk to the rendezvous; and will attend a performance of the Royal Ballet – three events that uncannily happen later that day, and lead to Steed being suspected of having killed Cowley, a clerk in the accounts department. Stanton's next prediction warns Steed that he will kill Wigmore, an accountant brought into investigate the department finances. Steed agrees to meet Wigmore but is clubbed down from behind and when Wigmore's dead body is discovered and the gun in Steed's hand proves to be the murder weapon, Steed is put under house arrest pending further investigation. Wallace and Richards continue to build up the evidence against Steed and arrange to have a large amount of cash deposited in the agent's night safe. Gambit, forewarned by Stanton of the event, is too late to stop the delivery being made and is forced to kill the man when he attempts to escape. Steed meanwhile convinces Purdey of his innocence, and promises that all will be made clear after he has broken into the paymaster's office that evening. He does so but, finding nothing, returns home.

Wallace and Richards decide that the time is ripe to play their trump card and have Steed's own gun left at the scene of Steed's death – his suicide will prove an admission of guilt. However, when Richards attempts to plant the weapon in Steed's home, the agent is waiting for him and places the man in custody. Purdey and Gambit arrest Wallace, who later confesses his guilt. When asked to 'forecast' the length of their prison sentence, Stanton falters before replying: 'How would I know.'

Gambit questions Victoria Stanton after a seance had forecast Steed's death in Medium Rare.

THE LION AND THE UNICORN

by John Goldsmith

John Steed	Patrick Macnee
Mike Gambit	Gareth Hunt
Purdey	Joanna Lumley
Unicorn	Jean Claudio
Leparge	Maurice Marsac
Henri	Raymond Bussieres

Directed by Ray Austin

STEED had insisted that the Minister wear a flak jacket. The expected attack takes place, but proves unsuccessful – the Unicorn's attempt on the Minister's life fails. Steed had come up against the Unicorn – a ruthless, brilliant killer and one of the world's top five agents with a triple D rating – before and he desperately wants to take him and his whole operation alive and undamaged. When Steed receives a tip-off that his quarry is heading for France, The New Avengers fly ahead and succeed in holding the man prisoner in his own penthouse apartment. However, suspecting that something is wrong when a prearranged signal fails to materialise, two members of his organisation stake out the building and, seeing Steed in the Unicorn's apartment, send a hail of bullets into the room. The bullets pass through a mirrored wall divider, shattering Steed's reflection and killing the Unicorn. To avoid open warfare, Steed decides to maintain the illusion that the Unicorn is still alive and throws a security ring around the building.

In return, the gang take a hostage of their own – a royal prince, abducted from a hijacked train. It looks like checkmate except that Steed has already played his king, so he decides to play for time and asks the gang for twenty-four hours in which to work out a swap-over agreement. Suspicious of the delaying tactics, one of the Unicorn's gang climbs down the building and, finding the Unicorn's dead body, races off to inform his colleagues. Gambit gives chase and waylays the man, but when he turns out to be both dumb and illiterate the Minister suggests that they should inform the gang of their leader's death and offer unlimited funds for the safe return of their hostage. Steed disagrees and says the exchange must go ahead as planned.

The gang are told to bring their hostage to the building and Steed informs them that the exchange will be made by having them place their hostage into an empty lift stationed on the ground floor, while he in turn will send down the Unicorn in a second lift. Matters become complicated, however, when Marco, the gang's spokesman, informs Steed that they have strapped an explosive device to the prince's body – a device that will be detonated at the first hint of a double-cross. Needless to say, Steed has 'rigged' the exchange and the prince is rescued unharmed, but not before Gambit and Purdey play a game of bluff and counter-bluff with the gang – a 'game' that ends explosively for the gang when Purdey displays her footballing talents and Steed inadvertently detonates the bomb.

In The Lion and the Unicorn, *Steed offers a fellow professional – the handcuffed Unicorn – a glass of champagne while Gambit watches warily.*

OBSESSION

by Brian Clemens

John Steed	Patrick Macnee
Mike Gambit	Gareth Hunt
Purdey	Joanna Lumley
Larry	Martin Shaw
General Canvey	Mark Kingston
Commander East	Terence Longdon
Kilner	Lewis Collins
Morgan	Anthony Heaton
Wolach	Tommy Boyle
Controller	Roy Purcell

Directed by Ernest Day

WHEN Purdey is asked to join Steed in a security team protecting an important delegation of visiting Arabs, to his astonishment she turns the assignment down flat. Unknown to her colleague, seven years earlier when Purdey had been a dancer with the Royal Ballet, she had met and fallen in love with Larry Doomer. They had planned to settle down and build a home, but that all changed when Larry's father, a troubleshooter with an oil company, had been killed by Arab soldiers. Larry had sworn revenge and, when his fiancée had been instrumental in preventing his assassination attempt, they had parted. Doomer had now become Squadron-Leader Doomer, the man in charge of the aerial demonstration for the benefit of the visiting delegation – the same crowd who murdered his father.

Steed insists that Purdey join him, and their arrival at the base is met with the news that the armoury store has been broken into. However, nothing appears to have been stolen – all the rockets are intact. As the agents cross to the display area, Purdey bumps into her old flame. The meeting is brief, and the girl gives Doomer the cold shoulder. The delegates watch as the planes swoop low over their targets and the rockets explode as planned – all save the rocket from Doomer's plane, which he later claims exploded in mid-air behind a thick cloudbank. In fact the rocket now lies half-buried in a sand dune, from which it is hastily retrieved by Doomer's aides, Kilner and Morgan. Doomer, still obsessed with avenging his father's death, intends to fire the rocket at the Houses of Parliament during the Arab delegation's visit.

Doomer now goes missing and, believing that he is using the intended location of the home they planned together as a base, Purdey pleads with Steed to give her five minutes alone with Doomer before they close in. Her colleague refuses her request and Purdey speeds off alone on her motorcycle – having first shot out Steed's vehicle tyres. Doomer is about to launch the rocket from its site in a dug-out as she arrives. Purdey pleads with him to think again but Doomer, playing on their past relationship, defies her to stop him and raises his automatic. A shot from Gambit finally ends their affair, and Doomer falls dead at Purdey's feet. Enter Steed who, leaping to safety, drives his vehicle over the dug-out as the rocket begins its ascent. The resulting explosion showers the agents with debris as Purdey, her face stained with tears, leaves the scene alone.

Purdey in flashback to 1970 in a scene from* Obsession *when she was waiting in her dressing room at the Royal Ballet for Larry Doomer, the man she almost married.

TRAP

by Brian Clemens

John Steed	Patrick Macnee
Mike Gambit	Gareth Hunt
Purdey	Joanna Lumley
Soo Choy	Terry Wood
Arcarty	Ferdy Mayne
Dom Carlos	Robert Rietty
Tansing	Kristopher Kum
Yasho	Yasuko Naggazumi
Marty Brine	Stuart Damon
Murford	Barry Lowe
Miranda	Annegret Easterman
Mahon	Bruce Boa
Williams	Larry Lamb
Girlfriend	Maj Britt

Directed by Ray Austin

ONE of Steed's field agents, Willie, manages to switch on a tracking device when he is shot while on a mission, and when Purdey and Gambit find him his dying words are: 'Williams ... drug drop ... Wednesday ... Windsor.' The New Avengers, together with Marty Brine, a CIA agent, are waiting when the drugs are delivered. During the resulting chase Brine is shot and the assassin falls to his death – the ten-million-pound packet of drugs lying at his feet. The delivery had been arranged by Soo Choy, a Chinese overlord, as part of his plan to impress the 'Syndicate' and enter the world of the highly profitable drugs trade. Now, however, Choy finds himself labelled 'dumbhead' by his intended partners and, desperate to regain his lost reputation, he plans to take revenge. Using Murford, a Ministry official, he transmits a special 'Red Alert' code to Steed's department – a code that sends Steed and his colleagues racing to a deserted airfield where they board a plane for 'Rendezvous' – a secret base to be used in a terrorist attack. The plane, however, is piloted by one of Choy's minions whom Gambit is forced to kill during the flight. The pilotless plane then crashlands in Choy's territory where, hearing news of the crash, Choy promises to give his syndicate friends the heads of his enemies.

Gambit is the first to recover consciousness and, finding that Steed's arm is broken, he improvises a sling. Then, armed with a home-made bow and arrows, the trio set out to play a deadly game of hide-and-seek with Choy's armed soldiers. After avoiding detection for some time and putting pay to a number of Choy's forces, Gambit is taken prisoner and brought before Choy who promises that his death will be a painful one.

The overlord has, however, reckoned without the resourcefulness of Purdey and Steed, who overpowers the leader of Choy's forces, dons the man's uniform and marches into Choy's headquarters with Purdey as his 'prisoner'. Choy's elation quickly turns to despair when Steed strips off his disguise and trains his rifle at the huge man's chest. Gambit seizes the opportunity to turn the tables on Choy, and as the trio depart with Choy in tow, a playful Purdey laughingly describes their catch as a 'real Chinese take-away'.

Gambit and Purdey, hot on the heels of Choy's Chinese minions in Trap.

HOSTAGE

by Brian Clemens

John Steed	**Patrick Macnee**
Mike Gambit	**Gareth Hunt**
Purdey	**Joanna Lumley**
McKay	**William Franklyn**
Spelman	**Simon Oates**
Walters	**Michael Culver**
Suzy	**Anna Palk**
Packer	**Barry Stanton**
Vernon	**Richard Ireson**
Marvin	**George Lane-Cooper**

Directed by Sidney Hayers

STEED has planned an intimate dinner for two. His attractive guest arrives and he prepares the claret for the table. The telephone rings, and a voice informs him that Purdey is being held prisoner – to prove the point, her car is now parked in Steed's garage. He is told to play along or Purdey will die. Furthermore no one must know – least of all Mike Gambit. Racing to his colleague's flat, Steed finds the place deserted and is about to leave when a phone call orders him to take £5,000 to a specified rendezvous. He follows instructions and returns home to await further orders. A lock of Purdey's hair arrives in the morning post, and after several more calls and rendezvous he realises that they have all been 'dummy' runs. The gang wants something else – but what? The answer is quick to arrive and he is told that unless he steals the secret plans for The Full Allied Attack, Purdey will die. Later that evening, he enters the Ministry and photographs the plans held in McKay's safe.

McKay's interest is aroused when he is shown film of Steed making a money drop to the 'other side's' post office. Aware that his colleague often plays his own game, he lets the matter drop without further action. Later, however, when he finds an envelope containing £5,000 in Steed's mail he decides to have Steed followed. Steed gives his 'shadow' the slip and returns home to await the gang's next order. The gang send a man dressed as Steed to kill one of McKay's agents and when his body is discovered with Steed's gun by his side, McKay orders Gambit to bring Steed in for questioning.

Gambit's confrontation with his superior turns out to be a showdown between the 'Master' (Steed) and the 'Pupil' (Gambit), and the young agent is left gasping on the floor as Steed leaves to take the plans to the gang's location – a disused funfair that serves as home for Spelman, a Ministry official who is the mastermind behind the plot. Steed and Purdey soon find themselves under fire as they try to escape until Gambit, having located the gang's hideaway, arrives in style – racing to the rescue in an empty Ghost Train carriage. The trio soon mow down the opposition and, leaving Gambit to fight the gang's toughest thug, Steed allays Purdey's worries when he explains that 'Gambit is capable of beating *anyone*' He does so – with style.

In Hostage, *Steed is told by McKay that there may be a traitor in their midst . . . a rotten apple in the security barrel.*

K IS FOR KILL
PART ONE: "THE TIGER AWAKES"

by Brian Clemens

John Steed	**Patrick Macnee**
Mike Gambit	**Gareth Hunt**
Purdey	**Joanna Lumley**
Colonel Martin	**Pierre Vernier**
General Gaspard	**Maurice Marsac**
Stanislav	**Charles Millot**
Toy	**Paul Emile Deiber**
Jeanine Leparge	**Christine Delaroche**
Kerov	**Sacha Pitoeff**
Turkov	**Maxence Mailfort**
Minister	**Alberto Simeno**
Waiter	**Jaques Monnet**
Minsky	**Frank Oliver**
Guard	**Guy Mairesse**
Secretary	**Cyrille Besnard**
Soldier	**Krishna Clough**
Salvation Army Major	**Kenneth Watson**
Monk	**Tony Then**
Penrose	**Eric Allen**

Directed by Yvon Marie Coulais

1965, and a young Russian soldier bursts into an old Nissen hut, mows down a Salvation Army band and makes his getaway by leaping over a perimeter fence. In the process, he stumbles to the ground and dies – his face has changed to that of an old man! Steed rings Mrs Peel and tells her it is a mystery they may never solve until ...

1977 and three workmen drive into a garage workshop in France. Within minutes they have been gunned down by a young Russian officer and the garage destroyed by a grenade. Mrs Peel rings Steed who leaves for France with Purdey and Gambit. The garage owner tells them about the attack and Steed believes it is connected with the incident in 1965 – but how? Suddenly, they are disturbed by a series of distant explosions and together with Colonel Martin, a French policeman examining the incident, they race off to investigate. They arrive to find a château under attack from mortar fire directed by a young Russian officer. Gambit downs the man and when they examine the dead soldier's paybook, they discover that the man is fifty-two years old. Within seconds, the youthful face ages and the dead man's hair turns white.

A second château comes under attack and the events are repeated when a young Russian soldier, captured during the fighting, also ages within seconds of death. His paybook identifies him as being sixty-five years old. The autopsy reveals that each of the bodies had something buried in their brain – something that appears to be a small radio transmitter. Events are complicated further when General Gaspard, an elderly French officer, believes that he recognises one of the dead men as a man he served with before the war – an assumption that Steed disregards as nonsense until a scar on the man's cheek proves otherwise. The dead man had received the scar from the Frenchman's sword thirty years earlier. As they prepare to depart, Steed receives a telephone call from Toy, the Russian Ambassador in Paris, and outside a new barrage of mortar fire rains down on the building.

K IS FOR KILL
PART TWO: "TIGER BY THE TAIL"

by Brian Clemens

John Steed	**Patrick Macnee**
Mike Gambit	**Gareth Hunt**
Purdey	**Joanna Lumley**
Colonel Martin	**Pierre Vernier**
General Gaspard	**Maurice Marsac**
Stanislav	**Charles Millot**
Toy	**Paul Emile Deiber**
Jeanine Leparge	**Christine Delaroche**
Kerov	**Sacha Pitoeff**
Turkov	**Maxence Mailfort**
Minister	**Alberto Simeno**
Waiter	**Jaques Monnet**
Minsky	**Frank Oliver**
Guard	**Guy Mairesse**
Secretary	**Cyrille Besnard**
Soldier	**Krishna Clough**
Salvation Army Major	**Kenneth Watson**
Monk	**Tony Then**
Penrose	**Eric Allen**

Directed by Yvon Marie Coulais

STEED is informed by Toy that a satellite has gone wrong and is transmitting a full-strength signal over France – a signal that is activating a secret unit of Russian commandos, codenamed 'K' agents, who were planted by the Russians years previously. He further believes that unless the men are stopped, it could result in the outbreak of World War 3. Sometime later, Colonel Stanislav, a Russian agent, visits the Russian Embassy and is informed by the Ambassador that the entire unit of 200 'K' agents have either been killed or taken prisoner. Unknown to the man, however, there were in fact 202 'K' agents – one of whom is Stanislav's father – and the Russian leaves the room smiling. Later that day the two agents, Turkov (Stanislav's father) and Minsky, emerge from their hiding place in a French distillery warehouse, seconds before Purdey and Gambit arrive on the scene. Stanislav, watching from the shadows, sees the two men make good their escape then returns to the Embassy. However, the Ambassador has received word that there are two further agents in the unit – agents that have been given a special mission. They must be stopped and Stanislav must be arrested on sight. Stanislav, however, orders the Embassy guards to arrest the Ambassador and the man barely escapes with his life. He races to inform Steed of his discovery and explains that the two remaining 'K' agents are to destroy two specific targets – men whose elimination would almost certainly plunge the world into war. Before he can give Steed the targets' names, the Ambassador is killed by a sniper's bullet. Steed, too, is hit, but the bullet is stopped by a cigarette case in his breast pocket.

Steed now calls a special meeting of all Government representatives, but fails to convince the men of the plot. He leaves, his only ally Colonel Martin. Gambit now visits the home of General Gaspard but is unable to stop Minsky from taking his life. Gambit kills Minsky and he too changes into an old man. Stanislav meanwhile meets his youthful-looking father and explains that now Minsky is dead his father must complete the mission alone. Steed and Gambit compare notes and arrive at the conclusion that Gaspard's death was a red-herring, intended to lead them away from the real target – the French President, who will be assassinated when he attends Gaspard's military funeral. However, the funeral has more than one dead body when Stanislav is killed by Gambit and Purdey, and Steed rings the death knell for Turkov.

Colonel Martin tells Purdey that he is just off to the murdered General Gaspard's funeral in this scene from K is for Kill.

Clowning around can be a very serious business for Purdey when international secrets are at stake in Three Handed Game.

COMPLEX

by Dennis Spooner

John Steed	Patrick Macnee
Mike Gambit	Gareth Hunt
Purdey	Joanna Lumley
Baker	Cec Linder
Talbot	Harvey Atkin
Karavitch	Vlasta Vrana
Koschev	Rudy Lipp
Patlenko	Jan Rubes
Cope	Michael Ball
Greenwood	David Nichols
Miss Cummings	Suzette Couture
Berisford Holt	Gerald Crack

Directed by Richard Gilbert

STEED had a healthy respect for X.41, the enemy agent codenamed Scapina, and at last it appears that he has made a mistake. The New Avengers are waiting as their Canadian contact parachutes in to reveal Scapina's identity. The man is gunned down, however, and all they find is a blurred photograph of a man leaving a large building – his face unrecognisable. Steed is contacted by Karavitch, a Russian agent, who informs him that he will hand over Scapina's identity for one million dollars. The rendezvous – Toronto, Canada. Arriving in Toronto, the trio check into an ultra-modern security building where Baker, the security chief, delegates two of his agents to accompany Steed when he meets Karavitch. But the meeting is blown and Karavitch is shot from a moving van, and when the marksman is taken to the security building he throws himself to his death from an office window. Purdey meanwhile is investigating the man's files in the building's basement control room – a fortress which can only be entered via a bullet-proof glass box in which identities are cross-checked automatically by the building's computer. Lost in her research, Purdey fails to notice when the doors of the room slide gently closed and the entire complex seals itself and starts to pump out the air.

It now becomes clear that the building itself – codenamed Special Computerised Automated Project Plan X41 – is Scapina and Purdey is now trapped in its innermost bowels as she runs from room to room desperately trying to find an avenue of escape. Locked outside and unable to break down the building's defence system, Steed recalls that though the building is locked tighter than a drum it must still accept mail to its basement Control. Armed with this knowledge, he begins to cram the post box with a lighter and dozens of boxes of matches. At first, Purdey is unable to grasp her colleague's motive, then realisation dawns and she gathers up dozens of envelopes and kindles a fire on the control room's conveyor belt. She soon finds herself showered with water as the room's sprinkler-system answers the fire alarm. The deluge overloads the computer's power circuit and the machine grinds to a halt as Steed and Gambit race to the girl's rescue under the cover of Steed's open umbrella, allowing Gambit to comment that he always knew that it would prove useful – one day.

Gambit finds himself behind bars and held by the Canadian police after a hectic car chase in Complex.

THE GLADIATORS

by Brian Clemens

John Steed	**Patrick Macnee**
Mike Gambit	**Gareth Hunt**
Purdey	**Joanna Lumley**
Karl	**Louis Zorich**
Peters	**Neil Vipond**
O'Hara	**Bill Starr**
Tarnokoff	**Peter Boretski**
Barnoff	**Yanci Burkovek**
Cresta	**Jan Muzynski**
Hartley	**Michael Donaghue**
Huge man	**George Chuvalo**
Rogers	**Dwayne McLean**
Ivan	**Patrick Sinclair**
Nada	**Doug Lennox**

Directed by George Fournier

THE New Avengers are in Toronto on a working holiday when they are asked to check up on Karl Sminsky, a Red Army Colonel and KGB agent who is rumoured to have spent two years in Siberia on a secret training mission and has now turned up in Canada again. Sminsky has arrived accompanied by two aides, but they seem to be behaving themselves. In reality, Sminsky has taken a training course with over one hundred and thirty men. That total had been reduced to two and, on their arrival, Sminsky and his aides had been followed by two security men, both of whom now lie dead.

Steed is informed of the security men's disappearance and sends Gambit and Purdey to check the countryside where their radios had suddenly gone dead. Meanwhile, Tarnokoff, a Russian diplomat, had made a formal protest about Sminsky's sudden disappearance, but Steed points out that as Sminsky is KGB he could be up to something Tarnokoff doesn't know about. Matters come to a head when Sminsky's men attack two young Canadians in a small store. The two youths are killed barehanded by Sminsky's cohorts and Gambit remarks that they are up against some very special people. Gambit and Purdey find the dead security men and are joined by Steed. They are about to depart when Gambit recognises two faces in a saloon car as it drives by. Leaving Gambit to chase the saloon, Steed and Purdey head in the opposite direction and locate Sminsky's training headquarters. They are taken prisoner and told that they will be used as 'human targets', but Steed and Purdey quickly write off the enemy and find a tape-recording made by Sminsky which points to the Russian's mission – to break into the Canadian Security Building and smash the master computer files, effectively putting back the Canadian security system by twenty years. Gambit meanwhile loses his quarry and finds himself arrested for carrying an unlicensed gun.

Steed arranges his release, and the trio head for a showdown with Sminsky and his men – a battle that is hard fought until the highly trained agents eventually fade under the onslaught from Purdey and Gambit. Sminsky, however, concedes that his 'pupils' put up a good fight and tells Steed and his colleagues that they now face the 'Master'. Needless to say, when confronted with Gambit's fists and Steed's steel-lined bowler, even the 'master' cannot overcome the inevitable, and Sminsky soon joins his colleagues.

EMILY

by Dennis Spooner

John Steed	**Patrick Macnee**
Mike Gambit	**Gareth Hunt**
Purdey	**Joanna Lumley**
Collins	**Les Carison**
Phillips	**Richard Davidson**
Miss Daly	**Jane Mallet**
Kalenkov	**Peter Torokvei**
Mirschtia	**Peter Arkroyd**
Reddington	**Brian Petchy**
Alkoff	**Don Corbett**
First policeman	**Sandy Crawley**
Second policeman	**John Kerr**
Mechanic	**Don Legros**

Directed by Don Thompson

STEED is determined to uncover the identity of the Fox, so when Purdey discovers that the villain received regular funds from Arkoff, a courier, The New Avengers lie in wait at the next pick-up point – a deserted boat marina on Lake Ontario. After a short time a water-skier makes a fast and spectacular pick-up of the suitcase carrying the money. The skier is Gordon Collings, a liaison officer between the British and Canadian intelligence services – a man with enough 'inside' knowledge to keep himself one jump ahead of any pursuer. The man is eventually cornered in a filling station, but makes good his escape in a car that is later found abandoned. There are no fingerprints, but Steed recalls that the Fox had leapt over the car's roof during his escape and believes there is the possibility of a palm print. Collings hears about this and moves into action as Steed, Purdey and Gambit return to the garage workshop – but the car has gone. It belonged to a Miss Daly and is no ordinary car but a family heirloom nicknamed 'Emily' by its owner, and she has collected it and taken the car for a service. Fortunately, the agents arrive at the very second that 'Emily' enters the garage car-wash, and the valuable clue is saved from erasure when a quick-witted Purdey leaps on to its roof as the giant rollers edge the car into the bubbling foam. Reasoning that it would be safer to drive the car direct to Forensics, Steed tapes his bowler over the palm print and the agents set off for a jaunty cross-country trek, with the Fox's men hot on their heels and determined to use every means possible to stop them.

The incident-packed journey leads Purdey and Gambit into a 'moonshine' drinking session; the Canadian police on the trail of a car 'last seen wearing ... a bowler?'; and to Emily herself guzzling gallons of home-made hooch until a barrage of mortar fire laid down by the Fox and his cohorts finally writes off Miss Daly's pride and joy. The valuable palm print is saved, however, and eventually leads the agents to their quarry.

The team repay their debt to Miss Daly by presenting her with a new vehicle, and the one remaining piece of 'Emily' as a memento. She in turn raises a few eyebrows when, correctly identifying the palm print on the memento as belonging to Collings, she informs them that she is quite proficient at reading palms, leaving the agents to consider whether their hazardous journey had really been necessary at all!

In* Emily, *Gambit is challenged to a duel by a burly still-owner who is fuelled by the home brew which Gambit needs to fuel his car.

FORWARD BASE

by Dennis Spooner

John Steed	**Patrick Macnee**
Mike Gambit	**Gareth Hunt**
Purdey	**Joanna Lumley**
Hosking	**Jack Creley**
Bailey	**August Schellenberg**
Ranoff	**Marilyn Lightstone**
Malachev	**Nich Nichols**
Halfhide	**David Calderisi**
Milroy	**Maurice Good**
Doctor	**John Bethune**
Glover	**Anthony Parr**
Harper	**Les Rubie**
Clive	**Toivo Pyyko**
Czibor	**Richard Moffatt**

Directed by Don Thompson

THE New Avengers join forces with Canadian agent Bailey when he receives a tip-off that someone is being dropped at dawn. Czibor, a young Russian agent, parachutes in on schedule carrying a package which he manages to hide before dying of gunshot wounds. When the package is unearthed it is found to contain a Mark VI printed circuit control unit – proving that the Russians have moved ahead in missile guidance. Steed, however, is more concerned by the words 'Forward Base' spoken by Czibor before he died. His puzzlement increases further when Bailey's body is recovered from Lake Ontario.

Leaving Purdey and Gambit on stakeout to see who collects the package, Steed re-buries the package and departs. Soon Halfhide, a known Russian agent, retrieves the package, makes his way to the water's edge, throws the package into the lake and leaves – followed by Gambit. Meanwhile, something odd happens on the edge of the lake and a local fisherman finds himself on dry land one moment and up to his neck in water the next. Purdey retrieves the package from the lake, but it appears to be a different model – a Mark V. Halfhide gives Gambit the slip and returns to the lake where Purdey is astonished to see the man jump in fully-clothed, only to reappear moments later wearing a dressing gown. Events become curiouser and curiouser: Purdey finds a bird's nest full of fish and, much to the amusement of the local populace, Steed goes fishing with a magnet. Something, it seems, is very odd about the place and Steed believes it is connected to Typhoon Agatha, which had hit the area in 1969.

While investigating the lake by dinghy, Purdey is abducted by a group of divers. She awakens in a strange underwater world – not a submarine but Forward Base, a place populated by Russian spies who, having built a small aquatic community disguised as a peninsula beneath the lake, are on constant alert for World War 3. Meanwhile, Steed's fishing expedition finally nets him a clue to the base and he informs the aquamen that unless they surface within minutes an anti-submarine flotilla will open fire on the base. Seconds later a surprised Steed watches as rows of enemy figures rise from the depths – closely followed by Purdey, automatic at the ready.

***Purdey looks stunning in this oatmeal trouser suit on the bonnet of her TR7. She wore the outfit in* Forward Base.**

PRODUCTION CREDITS

Series produced by
Albert Fennell & Brian Clemens

Music Composed by
Laurie Johnson

Production Supervisor
Ron Fry

Production Designer
Syd Cain

Story Editors
Bob Dearberg - Graeme Clifford
Eric Wraite - Alan Killick
Ralph Sheldon

Fight Arrangers
Ray Austin - Cyd Child
(Episodes 1 to 13)
Joe Dunne - Cyd Child
(Episodes 14 to 26)

Casting Director
Maggie Cartier

Fashion Co-ordinators
Catherine Buckley
(Episodes 1 to 13)
Jillie Murphy - Betty Jackson
Jennifer Hocking
(Episodes 14 to 26)

All 26 episodes produced by
Avengers (Film & TV) Enterprises Ltd
&
IDTV TV Productions
Paris

The Four Canadian episodes carried the following credits:

(Opening Credits)
Albert Fennell & Brian Clemens
Present
The New Avengers
in Canada

Associate Producer
Ron Fry

Production Designers
Seamus Flannery - Daniel Budin

Stunt Co-ordinator
Val Musetti - Dwayne McLean

Co-ordinating Producer for Avengers (Film & TV) Enterprises
Ray Austin

A Production of
The Avengers (Film & TV) Enterprises Ltd
&
IDTV TV Productions Paris
&
Neilsen-Ferns Toronto

Filmed on location in Canada

Emily carried an additional credit:
Produced in Canada by
Hugh Marlow & Jim Handley

AVENGERS INC
– the Avengers' reception in the USA.

Having secured a sale for the first filmed series with the American Broadcasting Company (ABC) the producers were faced with a problem – that of 'familiarity'. UK viewers were, of course, well-acquainted with the exploits of Steed and his female colleagues, but the Blackman series, though screened in Canada, had never been shown in the USA.

The problem was solved when Albert Fennell and Brian Clemens decided to shoot a special 'introductory' teaser sequence that was tagged on to the beginning of the American prints.

The sequence began with a man wearing a waiter's jacket, walking into view across a giant chessboard. Suddenly, he falls to the ground and we notice that he has a dagger inplanted into a 'target' motif on his back.

Enter Emma left and Steed right. They cross to the dead figure and Steed kneels to pick up a bottle of champagne from the dead man's hands. He smiles coyly at his partner as she deftly replaces a small-calibre pistol into the top of her black leather boot. Emma returns the smile as, in close-up, Steed fills two glasses.

Proposing a silent toast, they empty their glasses and, carrying the champagne, walk off into the background – cue *The Avengers* main title.

Throughout this sequence, the music builds to a crescendo of tenor drum rolls, while a voice-over narration informs us that:

'Extraordinary crimes against the people and the State have to be avenged by agents extraordinary. Two such people are John Steed, top professional, and his partner, Emma Peel, talented amateur – otherwise known as *The Avengers.'*

Contrary to popular belief, however, the show was not an instant success with the American public or critics, as the following reviews of the first episode screened in the US, *The Cybernauts* (28 March 1966) clearly show.

MIXED US RECEPTION FOR 'AVENGERS'
The Daily Telegraph, 30 March 1966

'*The Avengers* had a mixed reception at its first showing on American television last night. "A brutal British import with tongue-in-cheek humour" was one comment. "None of the flair of *The Man From Uncle,*" said the *New York Herald Tribune*. The *New York Daily News* said: "It's a fierce but intriguing who-dunnit."'

One day earlier, Vincent Canby, the *New York Times* critic, had said:

The American Broadcasting Company, whose stated intention is to bring as much newness and variety to the summer television schedule as we possibly can, last night unveiled The Avengers, *a British-made secret agent series. ABC is obviously pulling our leg.'*

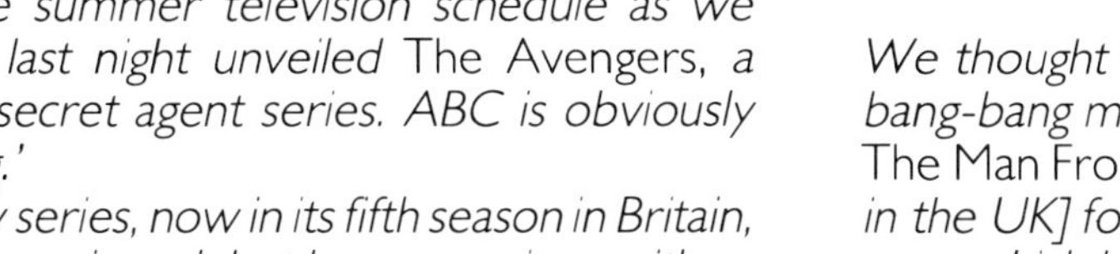

The weekly series, now in its fifth season in Britain, suffers in its American debut by comparison with so many other familiar shows that mix mayhem, mystery and comedy in approximately the same predictable proportions.

The faces on The Avengers, *belonging to Patrick Macnee and Diana Rigg, are new and attractive. However, no amount of 1966 dialogue about automation and transistors can obscure the fact that the formula was discovered during radio's early iron age – before showbusiness alchemists had turned Mike Hammer into the solid-gold James Bond.*

Indeed, in last night's adventure, The Cybernauts, it was never made clear whether the cool and clever Steed is a comparatively parochial private eye or a government agent with an international beat. It is the lack of such a fact that prevents a guy from really being able to identify.

The tale was unravelled at brisk pace and with just enough technical jargon to satisfy comic-book readers. To this extent, anyway, The Avengers *should be a diverting contrast to* Ben Casey *which it is replacing.*

Not all critics harboured this view. Harry Harris, of the *Philadelphia Inquirer* (29 March 1966) wrote:

We thought we were sated with secret agents and bang-bang melodrama – we haven't looked at even The Man From Uncle *or* Secret Agent *[Danger Man in the UK] for quite a while – but ABC's* The Avengers, *which bowed on Monday night, is a rrrouser!*

This British-made series, which has achieved great popularity there before the advent of all those other TV spy sagas, has several intriguing things going for it.

Patrick Macnee's John Steed is colourfully quirky. He wears Bat Masterson-type garb, including dapper derby [British bowler], totes a multi-purpose rolled-up umbrella and has an hankering for the old and elegant in clothes, home decoration and automotive transportation.

The tastes of his sidekickess, winsome widow Emma Peel, whom he always addresses as 'Mrs Peel,' although there are hints that they know each other quite well, are ultra-modern. She leans towards karate, sports cars and form-hugging black leather.

Honor Blackman, who first had this assignment, graduated to Pussy Galore in 'Goldfinger.' Now role and glistening togs are filled – fantastically! – by Diana Rigg. Her impact on male viewers. Bigg!

Chapter 1: The Cybernauts *profited from a taut, suspenseful and twist-studded script by Philip Levene, which began explosively with a series of single swat killings by an unseen, door-unhinging, wall-demolishing assassin.*

Before it was revealed that the skull-fracturer and neck-breaker was a robot controlled by a sick, sick scientist yearning for 'government by automation', there were intriguing detours into a karate class, a Japanese industrialist's office and a top company.

Roger the Robot zeroed in on his prey via radio-transmitter gift pens, and nonsense or not, tension built as the marked-for-murder Steed unwittingly handed this to Mrs Peel.

We thought he would save her in the nick of time by yelling something like 'Throw the pen out the window!' but a stand-up battle between the real *heavy-weights, Roger and another robot, provided a much more ingenious and exciting climax.*

Within six weeks, however, American viewers proved the critics wrong, and the American Broadcasting Company rang ABC to renew their option on further episodes. The rest is history.

Linda Thorson reflected in one of the mirrors of the light house at Peacehaven in Sussex during a break in All Done With Mirrors.

In How to Succeed at Murder, *Steed and Mrs Peel find themselves confronted by Throgbottom's minions in the keep-fit gym.*

In The Mauritius Penny, *Steed visits the stamp-dealer's shop and finds a clue to the killer.*

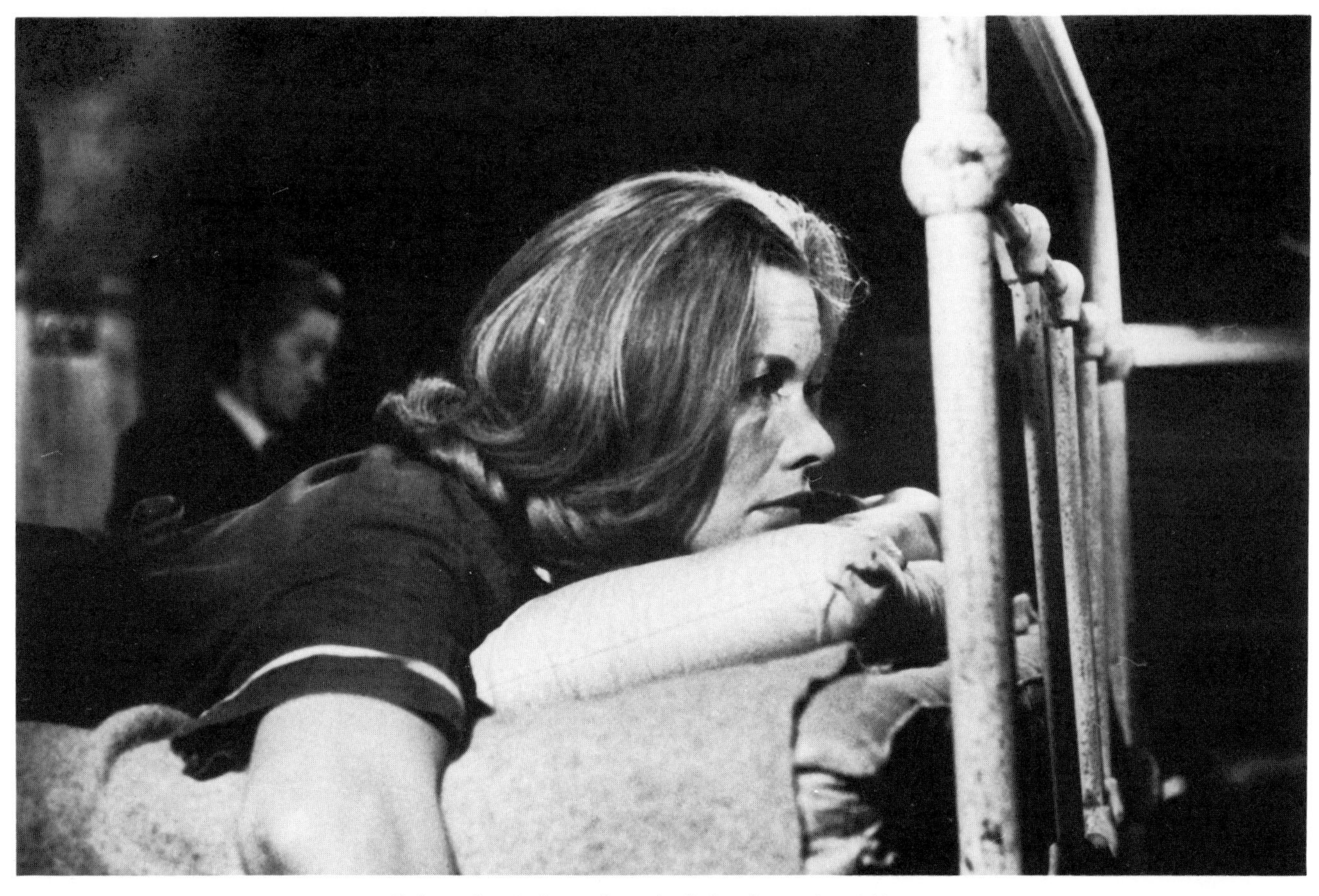

Cathy awakens in the condemned cell after the murder trial in The Gilded Cage, *and below in a thoughtful mood.*

A very unusual shot . . . Steed disguised as a vicar in The Little Wonders.

In the garden outside the peace conference building, Tara meets Steed, but is he the real *Steed – a scene from* They Keep Killing Steed.

*A rare pre-*Avengers *shot of Linda Thorson at a health and beauty farm during her toning-up period prior to hearing she had gained the part of Miss Tara King.*

Mrs Peel tries to avoid crossing swords with anyone in Honey for the Prince.

THE CURIOUS CASE OF THE COUNTLESS CUTS

Contained here are three selected extracts from the *Avengers* shooting scripts, reproduced exactly as they were issued, and complete with original spelling and other mistakes. Each extract has been chosen because I believe that it represents *The Avengers* at its very best and it helps to illustrate the vast number of production changes that were made during the actual filming of these (and no doubt all other) episodes prior to the televised versions.

On average, each shooting script contains around 130 scenes, 8,000-9,000 words and runs to 50-56 pages in length. Each dialogue sheet contains around 6,500 words and runs to 16-20 pages in length.

A short story synopsis appears next to each episode, and to help you understand the technical jargon used a full glossary of terms appears below.

The sharp-eyed among you will immediately spot major differences between the sequences reproduced here and the relevant scenes in the finished product. For example, the *Never, Never Say Die* extract is almost entirely different in content from the transmitted story, while *The Bird Who Knew Too Much* (Scenes 128 to 132 in particular) shows considerable variations in dialogue and continuity from the version that appears on our screens. Indeed, to my knowledge Scene 133 and the 'Tag Scene' sequence were never actually filmed. As with the previous Rigg monochrome series, it appears that it was the producer's intention to end each Rigg colour story by having Steed and Mrs Peel drive off into the sunset in various forms of vintage and/or veteran transport – hence the scenes slated to be filmed at Beaulieu House. Sadly, this idea was dropped, although various photo sessions were actually done in Beaulieu Grounds. The 'Tag Scene' sequence is, in fact, a rewritten sequence penned by the episode's author, Brian Clemens, who has since informed me that any script changes (rewrites) are first of all handed in – as was this sequence – on pink paper (scripts are printed on standard white bond) while any further rewrites are committed to green and finally yellow pages. The final brief extract illustrates the final scenes from *Game,* just before the Tag Scene. *Game,* in my opinion was one of the finest *Avengers* episodes made – I wish there was space to reproduce the entire episode.

There are many changes reflected in these scripts to the final, televised versions. I hope you enjoy this peek at the originals in all their glory.

GLOSSARY OF TERMS USED IN SCRIPTS

95 — This number denotes the scene being filmed (e.g. *Never, Never Say Die* Sc.95, is Scene 95) and is followed by the Director/Cameraman's scene identification in capital letters (e.g. INT. PASSAGEWAY RESEARCH UNIT. NIGHT = Interior shot; Passageway of Research Unit, Night-time).

DIR. CUT TO — Used to advise the editor/cameraman that this scene follows directly after the preceding scene.

ANOTHER ANGLE — Usually filmed by a second camera to give added dimension to scene being filmed.

FAVOUR — Cue for Director/Cameraman to elect to film this artiste/subject over others appearing in same scene.

CLOSE TWO SHOT — Two artistes are filmed side by side in frame (i.e. head and shoulders or full face shot).

C.U. — Close-up of artiste or subject in frame.

CLOSE SHOT — Alternative to above.

FADE IN — Scene fades in directly from previous scene.

FADE OUT — Scene fades to blank screen.

PULL OUT — Camera pulls back to reveal more of subject in frame.

LOCATION — Denotes where scene is to be filmed (e.g. outside studio).

HOLD THEM/HOLD — Camera is held on favoured artiste/subject for designated length of time.

INTERCUT — Cue for editor to edit various different shot/angles from scene for added effect.

Off/OFF — Item referred to (e.g. TV screen) but not actually seen in frame.

?VOICE — Character is not seen, but voice is heard over action.

REVEAL — Camera pulls back sharply to reveal subject.

ON — Camera focuses on one subject.

TAG SCENE — Final/closing scene of episode (usually with leading players).

NOTE — Scriptwriter's guideline to Director.

FINAL FADE OUT — End of Episode.

NEVER, NEVER SAY DIE

by Phillip Levene

John Steed	**Patrick Macnee**
Emma Peel	**Diana Rigg**
Professor Stone	**Christopher Lee**
Dr Penrose	**Jeremy Young**
Dr James	**Patricia English**
Eccles	**David Kernan**
Whittle	**Christopher Benjamin**
Sergeant	**John Junkin**
Private	**Peter Dennis**
Carter	**Geoffrey Reed**
Selby	**Alan Chuntz**
Elderly gent	**Arnold Ridley**
Young man	**David Gregory**
Nurse	**Karen Ford**

Directed by Robert Day
Produced by Albert Fennell
and Brian Clemens

Reports of a Frankenstein-like monster roaming the English countryside (and being frequently run down by cars and machine-gunned by soldiers – all without any fatal effect) lead Steed and Mrs Peel on a merry chase that eventually leads them to the Geoteric Research Unit, a top-secret establishment run by Professor Frank N. Stone and fellow scientist Doctor Penrose, who are, in reality, 'duplicates' of the two men.

Following numerous leads, Mrs Peel and Dr James, a hospital surgeon treating the monster's victims, are kidnapped, inciting Steed to follow Penrose to the research unit. Following a confrontation between Steed and Professor Stone (who reveals that Steed has been following a 'double' – a 'duplicate' Penrose), Steed produces his ministry pass and demands to be shown around the establishment. Stone leads him into an underground complex where the agent discovers his colleague and Dr James locked in a cell. Now read on ....

SC. 95. INT. PASSAGEWAY. RESEARCH UNIT.

The 1st grille is rising - STONE hurries into passageway past CAMERA - STEED following.

DIRECT CUT TO:

SC. 96. INT. STONES'S OFFICE. NIGHT.

C.S. PENROSE - TILTING DOWN from his face to arm resting on side of chair. Hand moves - slowly at first as it reaches over arm towards switch - Gradually fingers encircle switch - and turns it back slowly -

Oscillating sound recommences -

DIRECT CUT TO:

SC. 97. INT. EXPERIMENTAL SECTION. NIGHT.

Second grille is rising as STONE appears along passageway and enters experimental section followed by STEED.

STONE switches on light and hurries across to caged area. STONE AND STEED react to find EMMA AND DR. JAMES in the cage.

STEED

Mrs. Peel!

(To STONE)

Well ... if you needed confirmation ..!

STONE hastens to unlock the cage.

STONE

I can't tell you how sorry I am ... I trust you're unharmed?

EMMA

A little worse for wear, but no permanent scars!

(A smile)

Do we have a key?

STONE

Yes ... yes, of course ....

STONE withdraws key and inserts it in lock.

STEED sidles up to cage to join EMMA in CLOSE TWO SHOT.

EMMA
(lightly)
And how came we here?

STEED
(inclining head)
That's the real Doctor Penrose
you have in there.

JAMES
We gather that ....

STONE opens cage door.

STONE
There!

STEED enters the cage and regards the unconscious DOCTOR STONE.

STEED
Remarkable!

EMMA
(indicating MONSTER)
So's he! Don't you think?

STEED regards STONE's DUPLICATE. His face is damp with perspiration and is unshaven.

STEED'S eyes narrow - he exchanges a look with EMMA

EMMA
Yes, needs a shave, doesn't he?
But who ever heard of a robot
growing a beard!
(Indicating STONE)
There's your duplicate!

STONE in doorway reacts sharply to exchange - He makes a move towards cage door.

EMMA kicks at door before STONE can lock it. It swings open pinning STONE between cage and back of door.

STEED, JAMES and EMMA race towards passageway.

SC. 98. INT. PASSAGEWAY. NIGHT.

STEED, DR. JAMES AND EMMA continue to move speedily towards closed door at end of passageway. JAMES lags back - she stumbles - STEED turns to help her - but: grille descends between him and her - he spins round to see the other grille descending. He and EMMA are trapped between the two grilles.

STONE grabs JAMES - thrusts her back into the cell - slams the door on her - then turns back to passageway.

Meanwhile locks it, door at far end of passageway opens - PENROSE appears.

SC. 99. INT. PASSAGEWAY. NIGHT.

STEED AND EMMA are virtually in a cage - grille at either end - STONE one end - PENROSE the other.

STONE

We duplicates are programmed to survive, Mr. Steed. We are programmed to take over ..... Your Minister's will arrive for their inspection .... but duplicates will leave .... duplicates so perfect that they defy detection - such as these.

He pushes a button - a panel in the passageway opens up - to reveal:

CLONE SHOT. See COMPARTMENT behind panel - containing duplicate STEED AND EMMA.

NOTE - the compartment is in that section of passageway that EMMA & STEED are trapped in.

STEED AND EMMA react.

FAVOUR STONE - he calls across them to PENROSE.

STONE

Amusing, don't you think, Penrose? Our uninvited guests - destroyed by themselves!

He pushes another button - the FAKE STEED AND EMMA start to animate slightly - the fixed faces move a fraction.

FAVOUR STEED AND EMMA -
EMMA produces a tiny transistor radio - starts to tune it in.

STEED
(astonished)

Do you want the latest cricket scores?

EMMA
Frequency five, four oh!

The radio is ossilating - but EMMA has not found the frequency - when: FAKE EMMA lunges in - EMMA tosses the radio to:

STEED - who catches it - tries to tune it in. But he never makes it - the FAKE STEED lunges in on him - knocks his arm - the transistor flies away and :

ANOTHER ANGLE.
The radio skids across the floor - to end up close to the cell containing DR. JAMES - the radio is still whistling slightly - DR. JAMES eyes it.

ANOTHER ANGLE.
As FAKE EMMA fights EMMA - FAKE STEED fights STEED. It is a hard and difficult fight - because the FAKES do everything the real pair do - EMMA throws FAKE - FAKE throws EMMA in identical manner. Plus the fact that the FAKES appear invulnerable - it is a fight STEED AND EMMA cannot win.

STONE AND PENROSE watch - oblivious of the fact that:

DR. JAMES is stretching her arm through the bars - the very edge of her fingers touching the transistor - striving to bring it closer.

FAKE STEED AND EMMA fight real STEED AND EMMA. But STEED AND EMMA are fighting a losing battle - they cannot hurt the FAKES.

DR. JAMES has hold on the radio now - she draws it into the cell - starts to tune in the frequency.

STEED AND EMMA end up - back to back in the middle of the passageway - each facing their own FAKE - watching them move in for the kill.

EMMA
(breathless)

I can't stop me!

STEED

Me neither. I'm invulnerable.

EMMA

I can't be hurt.

The FAKES move in - and, at the last moment:

DR. JAMES finds the frequency - the ossilation builds - the FAKES react - their footsteps falter - they start to lose co-ordination and control of their limbs.

PENROSE AND STONE are equally affected by it - but STONE swings round to the cell - he fumbles for the keys to unlock it - to get into DR. JAMES and destroy the transistor. DR. JAMES draws back to the far side of the cell, holding radio - turning the volume full up.

STONE fumbles with the keys - finally finds the right one - but is unable to insert it into the lock - his control goes hay-wire.

THE FAKE STEED AND EMMA start to sway - to fall.

PENROSE has collapsed against the grille.

STONE drops the keys - tries to command his body to pick them up - but never makes it - he staggers away - falls against the switch controlling the grilles - the grilles start to rise.

STONE staggers once more - then falls heavily.

The radio blares on - PENROSE, FAKE STEED, FAKE EMMA AND STONE are disabled.

STEED AND EMMA move out - unlock cell and release DR.JAMES - STEED takes whistling radio from her - surveys the fallen duplicates.

STEED

I feel such an occasion demands a few words ....

EMMA

Better get out before the battery runs down.

STEED
(hastily)

Those are the words!

STEED, EMMA AND JAMES turn to move.

HOLD THEM. FADE OUT.

THE BIRD WHO KNEW TOO MUCH

by Brian Clemens
Based on a story by Alan Pattillo

John Steed	Patrick Macnee
Emma Peel	Diana Rigg
Jordan	Ron Moody
Samantha Slade	Ilona Rogers
Tom Savage	Kenneth Cope
Verret	Michael Coles
Twitter	John Wood
Cunliffe	Anthony Valentine
Robin	Clive Colin-Bowler
Mark Pearson	John Lee

Directed by Roy Rossotti
Produced by Albert Fennell
and Brian Clemens

Top secret information is falling into enemy hands and Steed and Mrs Peel have but one clue to the informant – Captain Crusoe, a parrot. A trail of birdseed leads the intrepid duo to Heathcliffe Hall, but alas, they find the bird has flown and is now being held by Verret, Cunliffe and Twitter, who have been using pigeons with miniature cameras strapped to their legs to photograph top-secret missile bases.

The agents are soon on their trail and, arriving at Heathcliffe Hall, they find themselves held at gunpoint by Twitter. Steed and Emma quickly overpower the thug and, stepping over his unconscious body, they enter a storeroom to find – Now read on ...

126. INT. REAR STORE ROOM. DAY.

CLOSE ON PARROT - as instantly it starts to talk:

"The deployment of the missle installation is in the main in the north western sector. There is evidence of advanced launching equipment. There are guider units of the X plus X variety - with a ranging self loaded, automated remote control guager unit of extreme complexity .. etcetera..etcetera...." This speech continues throughout the following.

STEED AND EMMA swing round - EMMA reacting big because - the parrot's voice has all the inflections of Cunliffe's speech.

EMMA moves closer to the chatting parrot.

EMMA
I know that voice...it's...
(remembers)
it's Cunliffe!

CUNLIFFE (off)
Cunliffe. Exactly, Mrs. Peel.

STEED & EMMA spin round to see CUNLIFFE, gun in hand, at the door. He glances down at the groaning TWITTER on the floor.

CUNLIFFE
I see you took care of Twitter for me. Poor old Twitter.
(smiles)
You hit the wrong man.

In background the parrot chats on.

CUNLIFFE

Better switch him off I think -

He leans forward, and with his gun, he bangs the traingle EMMA still holds - the parrot stops instantly.

CUNLIFFE
That's better. Now I'd better see about switching YOU off ... on a more permanent basis of course.
(hard)
Verret!

127. INT. REAR OF MAIN FOYER. DAY.

As VERRET steps out of concealment. He moves forward, gun at the ready.

He moves to the store-room door.

128. INT. REAR STORE-ROOM. DAY.

STEED & EMMA face the grim-faced CUNLIFFE and VERRET.

STEED holds his bowler - looks at EMMA.

STEED
Well - it worked once.

And instantly he lunges and chops with his bowler - chops the gun from CUNLIFFE's hand - and follows it straight up by charging him right in the chest - and out of the room.

At the same moment EMMA swings at VERRET with the triangle - hits him - sets him staggering (and, with the bong of the triangle, sets the parrot chatting on about missile installations again).

EMMA follows up - closes with VERRET - clouts the gun from his hand with the triangle (and shuts the parrot up again).

VERRET recovers - wrests the triangle from her hand - tosses it away (and sets the parrot off again).

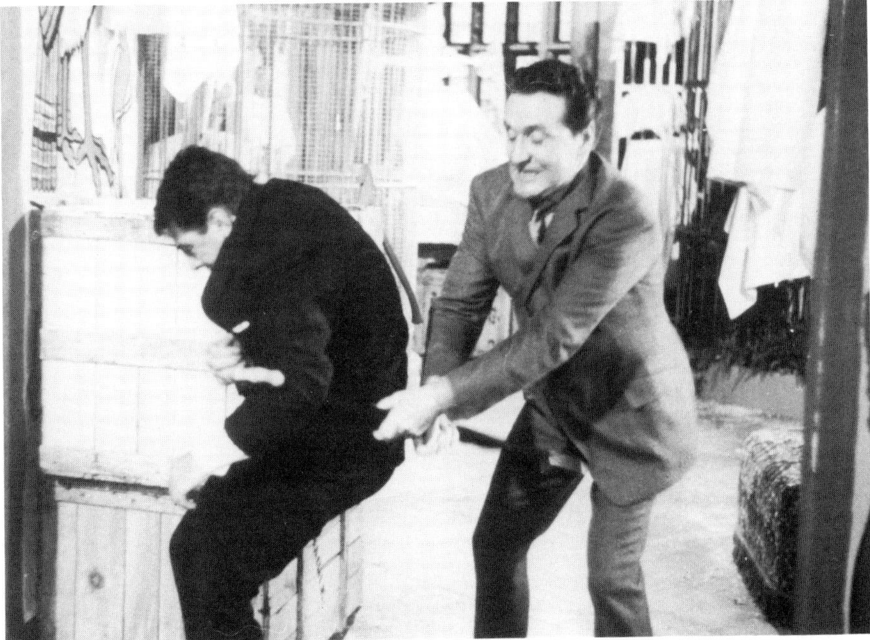

They fight across the room.

129. INT. REAR OF MAIN FOYER. DAY.

CUNLIFFE and STEED - STEED pursues him through the avenues of covered cages - then CUNLIFFE reaches a fire axe nailed to the wall - wrenches it free - whirls about just as STEED lunges in to grab him - CUNLIFFE swings the axe - STEED jumps back just in time.

STEED
Whoops!

CUNLIFFE pursues him back across the area now - swinging the axe - STEED keeps dodging - then suddenly he collides against a cage - the cloth falls off - STEED finds himself staring at a huge vulture.

NOTE: When STEED finds himself staring at the vulture:- should there be any difficulty in obtaining a live bird then we should go for (a) a stuffed bird or (b) a photograph.

STEED
Optimist!

Then STEED jumps aside - cleverly angles himself against a wooded packing case nearby. CUNLIFFE swings the axe - misses STEED - but his axe is embedded in the packing case.

CUNLIFFE desperately starts to tug it free - meanwhile - STEED, picks up a big cage full of tiny birds - and slams it down onto CUNLIFFE's head. To STEED's surprise, the cage not only knocks CUNLIFFE out - but the bottom breaks - so that the cage goes right down over CUNLIFFE - imprisoning his arms to his sides.

CUNLIFFE sinks to the floor 'wearing' the cage - the little birds inside it, flutter around his face, tweeting.

STEED smiles at the scene - then hears a crash off screen, remembers EMMA - turns and runs back towards:

130. INT. REAR STORE-ROOM. DAY.

As the feet of VERRET and EMMA kick the triangle and shut up the parrot again.

Then - PULL OUT - VERRET has EMMA in a strangle-hold - forcing her back, back - their feet again kick the triangle and set the parrot off again - then, EMMA reverses the hold, sets VERRET up for a prodigious throw - just about starts the throwing move as:

131. INT. REAR OF MAIN FOYER. DAY.

STEED running up to store-room door.

STEED

Mrs. Peel ... are you ...

He is cut short as VERRET flies out through the door at an alarming height - crashes into some crates and lies still.

An impressed STEED looks in through store-room door.

STEED (Contd.)

...all right?

132. INT. REAR STORE-ROOM. DAY.

EMMA on her feet - dusting herself down - the parrot chats on.

STEED picks up the triangle - bangs it - the parrot stops - then he moves to pick up the parrot cage - he and EMMA look at the parrot, exchange a look.

STEED

I think the powers that be will
be happy to know that we finally
got the bird ...

EMMA

(hastily adds)

Don't even say that!

HOLD ON PARROT.

FADE OUT:

COMMERCIAL BREAK

FADE IN:

133. EXT. BEAULIEU GROUNDS. DAY. (LOCATION)

OPEN ON the handsome RENAULT (1906) LIMOUSINE - standing waiting.

PULL OUT - REVEAL STEED AND EMMA - she gestures expansively towards the handsome beast - then moves towards it - STEED happily moves to enter the enclosed saloon of the car - he starts to close the door and settle down - then reacts as he sees:

EMMA is using the driver's compartment as a short cut - she is stepping right through the car - to alight the other side - and proudly waves her hand at:

The 1898 ROYAL ENFIELD QUAD - a tiny little two-seater bone shaker.

STEED - reacts - climbs out of the comfort of the limousine - and gets into the Quad machine. EMMA smiles - they set off - exit through the archway.

FADE OUT

INT. EMMA'S FLAT. DAY.

EMMA enters - notices the window is open - moves to close it - then (as in opening sequence) she hears something coming - ducks - something goes by overhead. EMMA swings round to stare at:-

AN ARROW imbedded in some object nearby. From it hangs a card.

WIDER ANGLE AS EMMA moves to take the card and read it. It reads:- "ARE YOU BUSY TONIGHT?".

EMMA reacts - turns to the window - and there is STEED - he leans into the room.

EMMA pings the arrow.

EMMA

I wish you'd get used to using the telephone!

STEED

Ran out of small change. Well - are you?

(EMMA looks questioningly)

Busy tonight?

EMMA

(warily)

What did you have in mind?

STEED

I'd like you to meet a bird.

EMMA

Will it talk?

STEED

Hardly. Not after it's been basted in red wine - turned twice on a spit - surrounded by pomme-a-la Grecque, and submerged under a fiendishly delicious gravy.

EMMA

Now that - sounds like MY kind of bird.

STEED

Be my guest.

He elegantly stands aside to allow her to exit through ..... the window.

HOLD THEM. FADE OUT.

GAME

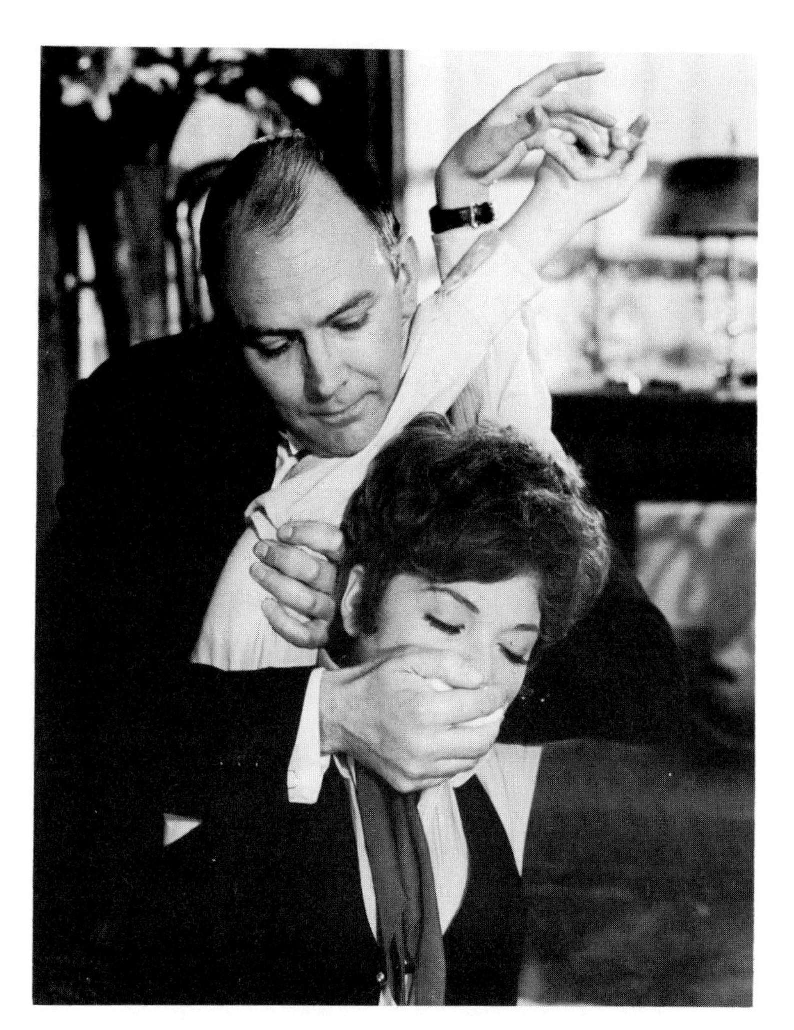

by Richard Harris

John Steed	**Patrick Macnee**
Tara King	**Linda Thorson**
Bristow	**Peter Jeffrey**
Manservant	**Garfield Morgan**
Professor Whitney	**Aubrey Richards**
Brig Wishforth-Browne	**Anthony Newlands**
Averman	**Alex Scott**
Dexter	**Geoffrey Russell**
Student	**Achilles Georgiou**
Manager	**Desmond Walter-Ellis**

Designed by Robert Jones
Directed by Robert Fuest
Produced by Albert Fennell and Brian Clemens

When several agents are murdered, Steed and Tara find themselves in possession of an abundance of clues – several hundred jigsaw pieces found on each of the dead men. When assembled, these reveal a picture of a house – a place they eventually learn is the home of a games king, Bristow. Unknown to Steed, however, Bristow is is fact one Sergeant Daniel Edmund, a man whose court martial for black marketeering was instigated by Steed in 1946. He is a man bent on revenge. The jigsaw pieces are designed to lure Steed into a trap and, when Bristow's manservant kidnaps Tara, Steed unwittingly walks into the spider's trap. We pick up the action after several near misses, Steed has managed to elude Bristow's best shots inside a giant games' complex. Now read on . . .

BRISTOW
(soft to
MANSERVANT)
This time we have him ...
this time ...

118. INT. GAMES AREA. NIGHT.

STEED inching along tunnel towards TARA at far end - he is thrusting his bowler ahead of him. We see it activate an electric eye cell - and instantly - a shiny steel blade clamps down, shutting off the view of TARA beyond.

119. INT. BRISTOW'S APARTMENT. NIGHT.

BRISTOW reacts.

120. INT. GAMES AREA. NIGHT.

REVEALING that STEED's bowler is cut in half - the steel blade starts to rise - TARA has gone.

STEED crawls out end of tunnel - holding half a bowler hat - he tosses it aside, looks around for TARA.

STEED
Miss King ... Tara!

And then he reacts to see six shiny bullets lying on ground nearby. He picks them up.

121. INT. BRISTOW'S APARTMENT. NIGHT.

MANSERVANT & BRISTOW

MANSERVANT
He's got further than
anyone, sir ...

BRISTOW
The game isn't over yet.

122. INT. GAMES AREA. NIGHT.

STEED hastily loading the empty ammo clip.

BRISTOW'S VOICE
The hardest part of the course, Steed. Six assailants at six second intervals.

STEED pauses in his loading - as he sees: SIX HUGE MEN standing in front of TARA in hour glass.

BRISTOW'S VOICE
Six, starting now ...

And the FIRST THUG comes charging down towards STEED - holding a long knife. STEED hasn't finished loading yet - the THUG charges in - STEED smashes him aside with gun butt - finishing loading and ramming clip into the gun - just as the SECOND THUG begins his run at STEED. STEED raises the gun.

BRISTOW'S VOICE
Oh, yes ... one thing I forgot to mention ... six bullets ... but only one is live.

STEED is icy cool - aiming deliberately at TARA's hour glass prison - seemingly oblivious to the huge SECOND THUG who charges down at him with long knife at the ready.

STEED pulls the trigger - once - twice - three times - the SECOND THUG is almost upon him - then: STEED gets the live bullet - gun fires.

TARA's glass prison is shattered - the sand starts to drain away from her face - she is free - meanwhile:

AT the instant of firing - the SECOND THUG has hit STEED - they go down together.

123. INT. BRISTOW'S APARTMENT. NIGHT.

BRISTOW reacting.

BRISTOW
Cheat. You cheated! You cheated!

124. INT. GAMES AREA. NIGHT.

STEED struggling with SECOND THUG. TARA free from hour glass now - and she runs in to start dealing with the other FOUR MEN.

BRISTOW'S VOICE
Cheat. Cheat. Cheat!

125. INT. BRISTOW'S APARTMENT. NIGHT.

BRISTOW rounds on MANSERVANT

BRISTOW
Get in there and stop them!

126. INT. GAMES AREA. NIGHT.

STEED and TARA have dealt with the THUGS and are taking a breather.

TARA
You did you know.

STEED
Eh?

TARA
Cheat.

STEED
Was always renowned for it ...
I recall a time at Eton when ...

TARA motions for silence - a door is opening - the MANSERVANT starts to enter the area - pushing gun in first. STEED & TARA exchange a look - each picks up a half of STEED's halved bowler - then each slams the two halves together - with the MANSERVANT's hand in between - then each slams a blow at him - and he goes back through the door into:

125. INT. BRISTOW'S APARTMENT. NIGHT.

BRISTOW reacts as unconscious MANSERVANT crashes into room - and STEED & TARA enter.

They come face to face with BRISTOW. He seems to have regained some of his composure now.

BRISTOW

Gamesmanship, Major Steed, I congratulate you. But you're not the only player who has a card up his sleeve ... one final trick ...

He quickly puts his hand up his sleeve and pulls out a playing card about twice the normal size. It is a black ace.

BRISTOW

The master card, Major Steed.

He runs the card along a leather table top. It cuts through the leather like butter. The card is razor-edged steel.

BRISTOW

The master.

Suddenly he flicks the card at STEED.

ON STEED

as he makes a backhanded tennis shot with what is left of his hat. There is a metallic clang, and:

ON BRISTOW

clutching his chest. The card protrudes from it. He staggers backwards.

ON STEED & TARA

STEED

Game, set and match.

HOLD THEM.

FADE OUT:

COMMERCIAL BREAK

TAG SCENE

Linda Thorson in a typically dangerous mood.

SEEING DOUBLE

Celluloid Mayhem to Order

Exciting and realistic action sequences punctuated every episode of *The Avengers* and, on countless occasions, the stars would be asked to perform a death-defying leap from a tall building; cling precariously by their fingertips to the bonnet of a fast-moving car; or leap from an out-of-control vehicle. Or did they? Of course not. The production company couldn't take the risk of having their most valuable assets – the stars themselves – injured by a mistimed stunt. Such an injury could have hospitalised the star for weeks or – in the case of a broken limb – months and added thousands of pounds to the production costs in delayed shooting time, not to mention the extremely high insurance premiums . The really dangerous sequences were handled by 'doubles', those unsung heroes of celluloid mayhem who ensure that the impossible appears believable – the stunt artistes.

Look again as Steed leaps to safety over the giant bulldozer blade in *The Fear Merchants,* or at Tara as she faces the motorcycle assailant before plunging from the clifftop in *All Done With Mirrors.* Perhaps the sight of Mrs Peel diving from the springboard in *The Bird Who Knew Too Much* quickened your pulse? If so, you're in for a surprise. 'Steed' was in fact Rocky Taylor, a professional stuntman who handled all of Patrick Macnee's stuntwork throughout the entire Rigg Episodes – a role he continued in *Invasion of the Earthmen* until the role of Macnee's double was handed over for the entire Thorson series to Paul Weston.

Cyd Child, a stuntwoman who specialised in doing thirty-foot leaps and falls from balconies, doubled Linda Thorson for the clifftop fight scene. In fact, this stunt was as dangerous as it looks and the motorcycle passed close enough to tear a few threads from her costume!. A regular with the series from 1965, Miss Child also handled all the 'rough stuff' for Diana Rigg. Close scrutiny will reveal that it is Cyd Child who manhandles the prison guard over her head before dumping him on to the bed in the scene from *The Living Dead.* Miss Child also took up the reins as fight arrranger for *The New Avengers* and did the occasional dangerous stunt for Joanna Lumley, although I have it on good authority that both Joanna Lumley and Gareth Hunt did about seventy per cent of their stuntwork themselves.

As for the diving stunt, it was performed by stunt*man* Peter Elliot! Peter also doubled Diana Rigg in the riverside action sequence in *You Have Just Been Murdered* and, dressed as 'Tara King' and wearing make-up and a wig, it is him we see doing the trampoline jumps in the opening sequence of *Have Guns' Will Haggle* – a stunt that went wrong and left him with a dislocated shoulder blade. Oddly enough, two other stuntmen, Gerry Crampton and Frank Henson – both *Avengers* regulars – doubled Linda Thorson in two other scenes from this story.

Even those breathtaking fight sequences were never quite what they seemed. They were meticulously planned by fight arrangers Ray Austin (the Rigg stories) and Joe Dunne (the Thorson stories), who led both the stars and their doubles through endless rehearsals until a no-holds-barred on-screen punch-up could look convincing and a punch, supposedly 'connecting' with a villain's jaw, in reality stopped fractions of an inch from its target. Then, by clever camera angles and post-production editing, the blow would appear to land on the designated area of the actor's body. Once again the stunt doubles handled the really rough stuff, while close-ups of the stars were later edited into the finished scene, leaving the viewer with the impression that they have just witnessed a full-blown encounter between star and on-screen villain. This, of course, is hardly 'cheating', for it is what appears on screen that counts. If a little bit of camera trickery adds extra sophistication to the proceedings we should perhaps offer our thanks to those 'unseen' heroes who, by their expertise, add that touch of realism to the action.

These days, of course, stunt artistes have gained some degree of recognition for their work and frequently receive on-screen credit for their input. However, this is quite a recent occurence and, as most television programmes produced in the Sixties and early Seventies seldom acknowledged them, here are the names of some of the many stunt artistes who made *The Avengers* one of the most exciting programmes of the last twenty-five years: Les Crawford, Eddie Powell, Cliff Diggens, Denny Powell, Bill Sawyer and Terry Richards.

Tara, contemplating the rules in **Game.**

DREAM MACHINES

Cars have always played a major part in the *Avengers* stories, and it is difficult to conjure up a mental image of Steed and his colleagues without recalling their personal mode of transport. Emma's powder blue Lotus, the red and maroon speedsters of Tara and the gleaming Vanden Plas lines of Steed's vintage machines - all have now become a part of the *Avengers* folklore.

It was not always the case, however, and though I am reliably informed that Steed drove a vintage vehicle (believed to have been a Vauxhall or Bugatti) in the latter part of the Blackman series, he was more likely to be found behind the wheel of a white Vauxhall saloon (registration number 7061 MK). His colleague, of course, professed a preference for two wheels – a powerful Triumph motorcycle (reg. 987 CAA) but she too could sometimes be viewed driving a sleek white MG sports. In each case, it is more likely that the cars had been 'driven' into camera range by the sweat and muscle of studio technicians. The series was, after all, taped live, and exterior inserts were kept to a minimum.

It is therefore fair to say that the cars reallly came into their own when, with the advent of the first filmed series in 1965, the creative brains behind the show decided to develop the idea of the stars driving a mode of transport that would, to some degree, reflect their own character traits. The ploy worked, and the cars quickly became a trademark of the series.

While everyone is probably conversant with the vehicles themselves, it appears that there is general confusion among the fans as to 'Who drove what - and where?' To that end, the following information should keep even the most avid and car-conscious fan satisfied.

Any attempt to list every vehicle used in the series would prove over-exhaustive, so I propose to limit my comments to the vehicles used by the stars themselves. As I do not profess to any expertise on the subject, I have resisted the urge to list each vehicle's technical data.

Each vehicle's registration number is followed by a bracketed single number or group of numbers. These denote the episode in which that vehicle appeared, and should be used in conjunction with the corresponding episode numbers listed between pages 82 and 90.

Emma Peel's blue Lotus Elan S2.

Steed's 1927 Rolls Royce, KK 4976.

THE AVENGERS

Model	Reg No	Comments
EMMA		
Powder blue Lotus Elan S2	HNK 999C	Throughout b/w series
Powder blue Lotus Elan S2	SJH 499D	Throughout entire colour series
STEED		
Green 1929 Speed Six Bentley	XT 2273	Throughout the b/w Rigg episodes
Green 1926 4½ litre Bentley	UW 4887	Throughout the b/w Rigg series and episode (20) Rigg colour
Green 1928 Green Label Bentley	YK 6871	Rigg colour (1)[1]
Green 1926 Speed Six Bentley	RX 6180	(2-5-6-7-8-11-14-16-18-19-21) Rigg colour[2]
Green 1927 4½ litre Bentley	YT 3942	(22-24-25) Rigg colour and (3-4-6) Thorson[3]
Yellow 1927 Rolls Royce Silver Ghost	KK 4976	(5-7-8 to 14 16 to 26) Thorson
Yellow 1923 Rolls Royce Phantom Tourer Mk I	UU 3864	(27-28-30-31-32) Thorson[4]
Olive-green Land Rover	WX 887	(8-10) Rigg colour
Trojan Bubble Car	CMU 574A	(24) Thorson
TARA		
Maroon AC Cobra 428	LPH 800D	(1 to 4 7-8-9-12) Thorson[5]
Red Lotus Europa	PPW 999F	(6-11 14 to 33) Thorson
Mini Moke	LYP 794D	(10) Thorson
MOTHER		
Silver grey Rolls Royce	3 KHM	(30) Thorson
Brown Mini Moke	THX 77F	(26) Thorson
LADY DIANA		
White MGB	BWM 300G	(19) Thorson

THE NEW AVENGERS

Model	Reg No	Comments
STEED		
Olive-green 5.3 litre Jaguar Coupé	NVK 60P	Throughout the first 13 stories
Yellow Rover saloon	WOC 229P	Several episodes of the second 13 stories
Green Range Rover	TXC 922J	Several episodes of the series
GAMBIT		
Red Jaguar XJS	MLR 875P	Throughout the series
White Range Rover	LOK 537P	Several episodes of the series
PURDEY		
Yellow MGB Drophead Sports	MOC 232P	First 13 stories
Yellow Triumph TR7	OGW 562R	Several episodes of the second 13 stories
Yellow/Black Honda motorcycle	LLC 950P	Episode (5)
Red Honda motorcycle	OLR 471P	Episode (18)

The stars also drove various locally obtained vehicles in the episodes made in location in France and Canada.

1 This model was featured regularly in the 1967 situation comedy series *George and the Dragon* starring Sid James and Peggy Mount.

2 In January 1984 this 1926 Speed Six changed hands for £49,500.

3 Eight years later, this machine made a 'guest' appearance in the *New Avengers* story: *K is for Kill*.

4 Familiar? It should be. This model frequently turned up in both *The Benny Hill Show* and *The Morecambe and Wise* programmes.

5 Steed in a low-slung sports car? That might have been the case. The AC Cobra 428 was, in fact, pencilled in to be the agent's regular transport throughout the entire Thorson series. Thankfully, the producers decided to retain his vintage image.

The 1929 Bentley, XT 2273, from a scene in The Gravediggers

Cathy Gale joins a motorcycle gang in Build a Better Mousetrap.

Tara's Lotus Europa, PPW 999F.

THE AVENGERS CHRONOLOGY

One question above all others frequently appears in my correspondence with *Avengers* fandom. What is the correct chronological order of the episodes, that is, the order in which the episodes were filmed or, in the case of the Blackman series, videotaped? (The Hendry series was, of course, transmitted live.)

Researching such a subject is seldom straightforward – it demands that the result achieved from such research can be considered as 100% correct – and was, I confess, undertaken with trepidation. It is, after all, over sixteen years since *The Avengers* ceased production; researching something of that age is almost entirely dependent on the goodwill and co-operation of the production company and/or production personnel. Fortunately, the production company was both helpful and unselfish in allowing me access to relevant paperwork, though I admit that I was somewhat dismayed to find that the majority of production files (namely the material relating to the Rigg monochrome series) was thin on the ground or was 'lost' and gathering dust on the studio's shelves.

Faced with such a situation, I requested and received further reference material from the production company and, surrounded by this (and mountainous piles of press review material), I whittled it down to something that resembles a true and complete picture of the Rigg monochrome filmed order.

As to whether the entire order contained here is free from errors, suffice to say that the information on the entire Blackman and Rigg colour series and on the Thorson episodes has been taken directly from the day-to-day progress reports files and can be taken as 99% correct. However, the information on the Rigg monochrome section is based on my own research and the production order as recounted by production personnel. It should, therefore, be taken as the probable production order and has been printed without confirmation. Admittedly, this may raise a few questions regarding the order in which the episodes were screened in the USA. (*The Town of No Return* turns up as episode 23, while *The Murder Market* story is placed at number 9.) However, as Brian Clemens has confirmed that the former had been completed and the latter was two-thirds complete before Elizabeth Shepherd was replaced by Diana Rigg, I believe it safe to assume that these two stories were the first to be remade when Diana Rigg inherited the role of Emma Peel, and the USA transmission order can be taken as confirmation that television companies seldom – if ever – screen any series in its correct production order.

Fortunately, if one discounts *The Forget-Me-Knot,* which was written to introduce the Tara King character and say goodbye to Mrs Peel, the *Avengers* series has no on-going continuity and it matters little in which order they are screened – or for that matter viewed – although I suspect that the following information will upset quite a few video indexes!

Wherever possible (that is, with the exception of the Rigg monochrome series, and episodes 1 through 9 of the Rigg colour series – for which production dates were not available) I have given two sets of dates. The date in the first column after the episode's title denotes the day/month/year that that episode completed production (prior to post-syncing and editing), while the right-hand dates denote the first transmission date of each UK transmission – based on the Central and Granada regions.

One final point of interest: although the average production time allowed for filming each story was ten days, almost the entire Rigg colour series and the Thorson episodes ran over schedule and the majority of the episodes were in fact filmed over twelve days, though a few actually took fifteen days to film.

In Pandora, *'Mother' (Patrick Newell) and Rhonda (Rhonda Parker) are astonished when Steed produces a note that fell from Tara's pocket which points to her abductor being the 'Fierce Rabbit' – a British agent in World War I.*

21

MACNEE/BLACKMAN SERIES 1

	Title	Production completed	Transmission date
1	Dead on Course	9/5/62	29/12/62
2	Mission to Montreal	12/5/62	27/10/62
3	The Sell Out	9/6/62	24/11/62
4	Death Dispatch[1]	23/6/62	22/12/62
5	Warlock[2]	7/7/62	26/1/63
6	Propellant 23	21/7/62	6/10/62
7	Mr Teddy Bear	4/8/62	29/9/62
8	The Decapod	12/8/62	13/10/62
9	Bullseye	20/9/62	20/10/62
10	The Removal Men	4/10/62	3/11/62
11	The Mauritius Penny	18/10/62	10/11/62
12	Death of a Great Dane[3]	1/11/62	17/11/62
13	Death on the Rocks	15/11/62	1/12/62
14	Traitor in Zebra	29/11/62	8/12/62
15	The Big Thinker	13/12/62	15/12/62
16	Intercrime	29/12/62	5/1/63
17	Immortal Clay	10/1/63	12/1/63
18	Box of Tricks	17/1/63	19/1/63
19	The Golden Eggs	31/1/63	2/2/63
20	School for Traitors	9/2/63	9/2/63
21	The White Dwarf	16/2/63	16/2/63
22	Man in the Mirror	22/2/63	23/2/63
23	A Conspiracy of Silence	1/3/63	2/3/63
24	A Chorus of Frogs	8/3/63	9/3/63
25	Six Hands across the Table	15/3/63	16/3/63
26	Killerwhale	22/3/63	23/3/63

1 Although this was the first televised episode starring Honor BLackman as Mrs Catharine Gale . . .

2 . . . this story was written as the first Mrs Gale story and the script contains scenes and dialogue between Steed And Cathy during their first meeting (at the British Museum). However, these scenes were inexplicably edited out of the transmitted story and I can only assume that as the previous episode was transmitted one week before this story, the producers felt there was little point in screening an 'introductory' story.

3 This story (with slight script changes) was later remade as *The £50,000 Breakfast* (Rigg colour series 1, episode 20) . . .

In Death of a Great Dane, *Steed is convinced that Getz is unloading Litoff's assets, and sends Cathy to investigate.*

Cathy receives a statement, and Steed is delighted to hear that her shares are now showing a handsome profit in Bullseye.

Steed and Cathy, handcuffed together by the enemy, receive a consoling visit in Dressed to Kill.

MACNEE/BLACKMAN SERIES 2

	Title	Production completed	Transmission date
1	Concerto	26/4/63	2/3/64
2	Brief for Murder	1/5/63	28/9/63
3	The Nutshell	10/5/63	19/10/63
4	The Golden Fleece	24/5/63	7/12/63
5	Death à la Carte	14/6/63	21/12/63
6	Man With Two Shadows	21/6/63	12/10/63
7	Don't Look Behind You[4]	5/7/63	14/12/63
8	The Grandeur That Was Rome	19/7/63	30/11/63
9	The Undertakers	2/8/63	5/10/63
10	Death of a Batman	14/8/63	26/10/63
11	Build a Better Mousetrap	28/8/63	15/2/64
12	November Five	27/9/63	2/11/63
13	Second Sight	11/10/63	16/11/63
14	The Secret's Broker	19/10/63	1/2/64
15	The Gilded Cage	25/10/63	9/11/63
16	The Medicine Men	8/11/63	23/11/63
17	The White Elephant	22/11/63	4/1/64
18	Dressed to Kill	6/12/63	28/12/63
19	The Wringer	20/12/63	18/1/64
20	The Little Wonders	3/1/64	11/1/64
21	Mandrake	16/1/64	25/1/64
22	The Trojan Horse	30/1/64	8/2/64
23	The Outside-In Man	12/2/64	22/2/64
24	The Charmers	27/2/64	29/2/64
25	Esprit de Corps	11/3/64	14/3/64
26	Lobster Quadrille[5]	20/3/64	21/3/64

4 . . . as was this story, which served as the plot for *The Joker* (Rigg colour series 1, episode 15).

5 As this episode heralded the departure of Honor Blackman as Cathy Gale, the final scenes (in which Cathy has supposedly been burned to death) remained a well-kept studio secret until the episode was transmitted. In reality, Steed explained Cathy's absence by remarking that 'I've no doubt that she is pussy-footing around on some foreign island!' (Honor was, by this time, playing Pussy Galore in the James Bond film *Goldfinger*.

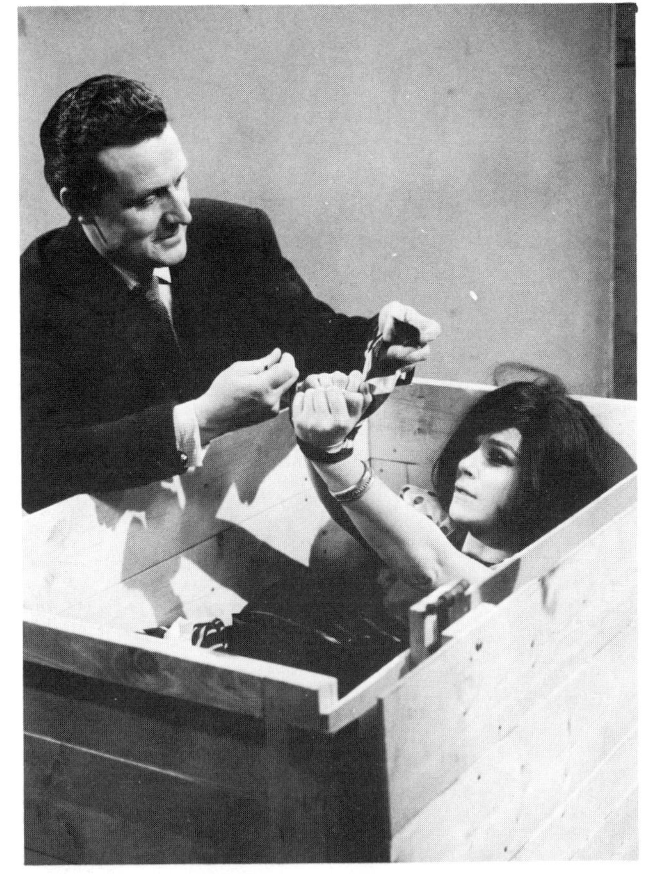

Steed releases the bound and gagged Kim Lawrence (Fenella Fielding) from a crate in The Charmers.

A publicity shot that illustrates the charms of Honor Blackman and the character of Cathy Gale.

MACNEE/RIGG MONOCHROME SERIES

		Production completed	Transmission date
1	The Town of No Return	Not known	2/10/65
2	The Murder Market	n/k	13/11/65
3	The Gravediggers	n/k	9/10/65
4	The Cybernauts	n/k	16/10/65
5	Death at Bargain Prices	n/k	23/10/65
6	Castle De'Ath	n/k	30/10/65
7	The Master Minds	n/k	6/11/65
8	A Surfeit of H_2O	n/k	20/11/65
9	The Hour that Never Was	n/k	27/1/65
10	Dial a Deadly Number	n/k	4/12/65
11	The Maneater of Surrey Green	n/k	11/12/65
12	Two's a Crowd	n/k	18/12/65
13	Too Many Christmas Trees	n/k	25/12/65
14	Silent Dust	n/k	1/1/66
15	Small Game for Big Hunters	n/k	15/1/66
16	Room Without a View	n/k	8/1/66
17	The 13th Hole	n/k	29/1/66
18	The Girl from Auntie	n/k	21/1/66
19	The Quick, Quick Slow Death	n/k	5/2/66
20	The Danger Makers	n/k	12/2/66
21	A Touch of Brimstone	n/k	19/2/66
22	What the Butler Saw	n/k	26/2/66
23	A Sense of History	n/k	12/3/66
24	The House that Jack Built	n/k	5/3/66
25	How to Succeed at Murder		
	Without Really Trying	n/k	19/3/66
26	Honey for the Prince	n/k	23/3/66

A black-and-white crepe catsuit designed by John Bates looks especially appealing when modelled by Diana Rigg.

It's hardly cricket, as Steed returns the deadly knives thrown by Wentworth's henchmen in Death at Bargain Prices.

A splendid shot of Emma Peel dressed as Robin Hood in A Sense of History.

Emma peers through the giant portrait of herself which she finds in the exhibition room of the strange house in which she is held prisoner in The House that Jack Built.

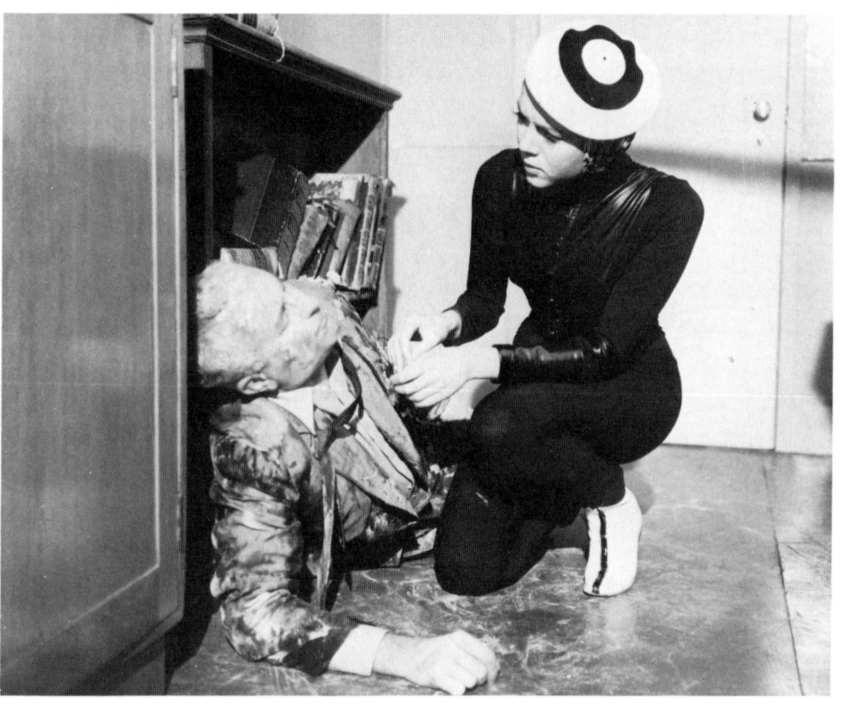

Emma arrives at the village church to discover that both the parish records and the vicar have been 'rubbed out' in The town of No Return.

Emma is all trussed up and nowhere to go in The Town of No Return.

MACNEE/RIGG COLOUR SERIES 1

	Title	Production completed	Transmission date
1	The Fear Merchants	Not known	21/1/67
2	Escape in Time	n/k	28/1/67
3	The Bird Who Knew Too Much	n/k	11/2/67
4	From Venus With Love	n/k	14/1/67
5	The See-Through Man	n/k	4/2/67
6	The Winged Avenger	n/k	18/2/67
7	The Living Dead	n/k	25/2/67
8	The Hidden Tiger	n/k	4/3/67
9	The Correct Way to Kill	n/k	11/3/67
10	Never, Never Say Die	14/2/67	18/3/67
11	Epic	27/2/67	1/4/67
12	The Superlative Seven	13/3/67	8/4/67
13	A Funny Thing Happened		
	on the Way to the Station	22/3/67	15/4/67
14	Something Nasty in the Nursery	2/4/67	22/4/67
15	The Joker	11/4/67	29/4/67
16	Who's Who?	18/4/67	6/5/67
17	Death's Door	7/6/67	7/10/67
18	Return of the Cybernauts	15/6/67	30/9/67
19	Dead Man's Treasure	5/7/67	21/10/67
20	The £50,000 Breakfast	20/7/67	14/10/67
21	You Have Just Been Murdered	2/8/67	28/10/67
22	The Positive Negative Man	31/8/67	4/11/67
23	Murdersville	25/8/67	11/11/67
24	Mission Highly Improbable	22/9/67	18/11/67
25	The Forget-Me-Knot[6]	19/1/68	12/1/69

6 This episode is included in both lists for completeness and though it actually appears on the production company's records as the final Rigg story, it is, of course, widely considered to be the first Thorson story. In fact, this episode was filmed between December 1967 and January 1968, while the crossover scene between Emma and Tara was actually filmed on 19 January 1968.

MACNEE/THORSON COLOUR SERIES 2

	Title	Production completed	Transmission date
1	Invasion of the Earthmen	21/11/67	27/4/69
2	The Curious Case of		
	the Countless Clues	19/1/68	18/5/69
3	The Forget-Me-Knot	19/1/68	12/1/69
4	Split	1/2/68	9/2/69
5	Getaway	15/2/68	27/7/69
6	Have Guns Will Haggle[7]	29/2/68	30/3/69
7	Look, Stop Me If You've		
	Heard This One Before		
	(But There Were These)	19/3/68	23/3/69
8	My Wildest Dream	1/4/68	7/9/69
9	Whoever Shot Poor George		
	Oblique Stroke XR40	17/4/68	16/2/69
10	You'll Catch Your Death	24/5/68	2/2/69
11	All Done With Mirrors	13/6/68	2/3/69
12	The Super Secret		
	Cypher Snatch	14/6/68	26/1/69
13	Game	25/6/68	19/1/69
14	False Witness	11/7/68	23/2/69
15	Noon Doomsday	30/7/68	16/3/69
16	Legacy of Death	9/8/68	9/3/69
17	They Keep Killing Steed	29/8/68	6/4/69
18	Wish You Were Here	12/9/68	25/5/69
19	Killer	27/9/68	4/5/69
20	The Rotters	8/10/68	20/4/69
21	The Interrogators	22/10/68	13/4/69
22	The Morning After	5/11/68	11/5/69
23	Love All	18/11/68	13/7/69
24	Take Me To Your Leader	29/11/68	15/6/69
25	Stay Tuned	13/12/68	8/6/69
26	Fog	31/12/68	23/6/69
27	Who Was That Man		
	I Saw You With?	10/1/69	31/8/69
28	Pandora	17/1/69	10/8/69
29	Thingumajig	21/1/69	1/8/69
30	Homicide and Old Lace[8]	23/1/69	6/7/69
31	Requiem	13/2/69	17/8/69
32	Take Over	21/2/69	24/8/69
33	Bizarre	3/3/69	14/9/69

Trapped in a church crypt, Tara escapes by using the case's self-destructing device to open the crypt door in this scene from Take Me To Your Leader.

7 This episode is actually a remake of the story entitled *Invitation to a Killing* which, though filmed as the very first Thorson story (Oct/Nov 1967), was thrown out as unsuitable by Albert Fennell and Brian Clemens when they returned to head the production team as joint producers. Close scrutiny of this episode clearly reveals that several of the scenes filmed for the first story were used in *Have Guns, Will Haggle.* (Note the seasonal changes from autumn to summer.)

Incidentally, an interesting point is that Jennifer Croxton, (later to play Lady Diana Forbes-Blakeney in *Killer*) appears in the cast list for the original story – although she didn't, of course, appear in the remake.

I have been unable to ascertain why the original episode was scrapped, and can only assume that Albert Fennell and Brian Clemens felt that it wasn't up to their usual high standards – a fate that also befell . . .

8 . . . *The Great, Great Britain Crime* – a story that, though filmed third in the Thorson chronological order (and completed on 6 December 1967), was also scrapped but later used as the central plot for Mother's birthday story in *Homicide and Old Lace.*

Steed, Inge (Dora Reisser) and Teddy Shelley (Jeremy Lloyd) survey the oddments that have been dredged from the river in their search for the black box in Thingumajig.

In The Curious Case of the Countless Clues, *Stanley (Tony Selby) meets harsh justice from Steed when he tries to frame the agent.*

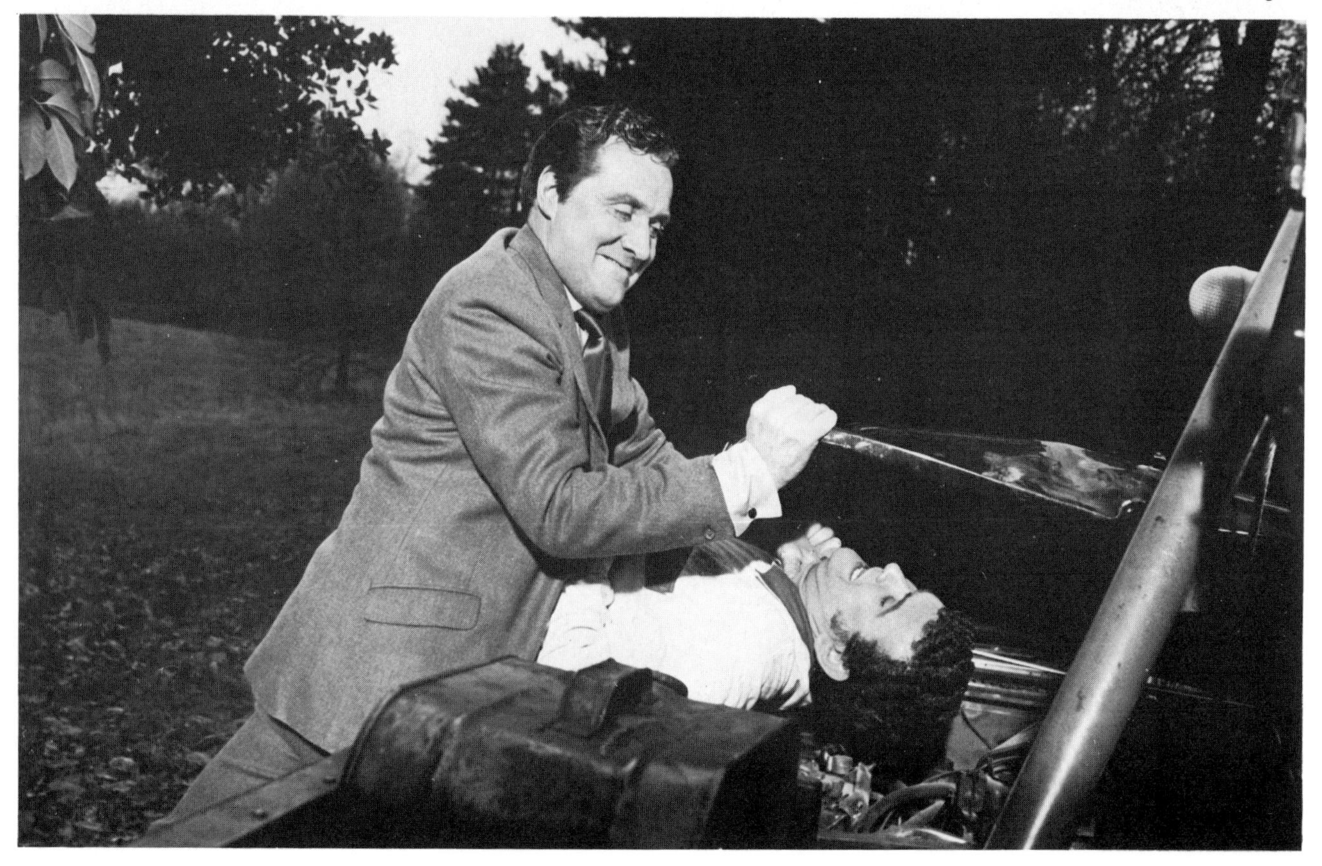

Cornered in the hayloft by Grant, Tara turns the tables, gains his gun and shoots him – a scene from Noon Doomsday.

A helping hand from Tara for Steed who, leg in plaster, is at a distinct disadvantage as they wait for Kafta's arrival in Noon Doomsday.

Tara throws Sweeno (Joe Dunne) down the lighthouse steps – all 365 of them – in All Done With Mirrors.

Steed finds Tara in what appears to be a hypnotic trance from this scene from The Super Secret Cypher Snatch.

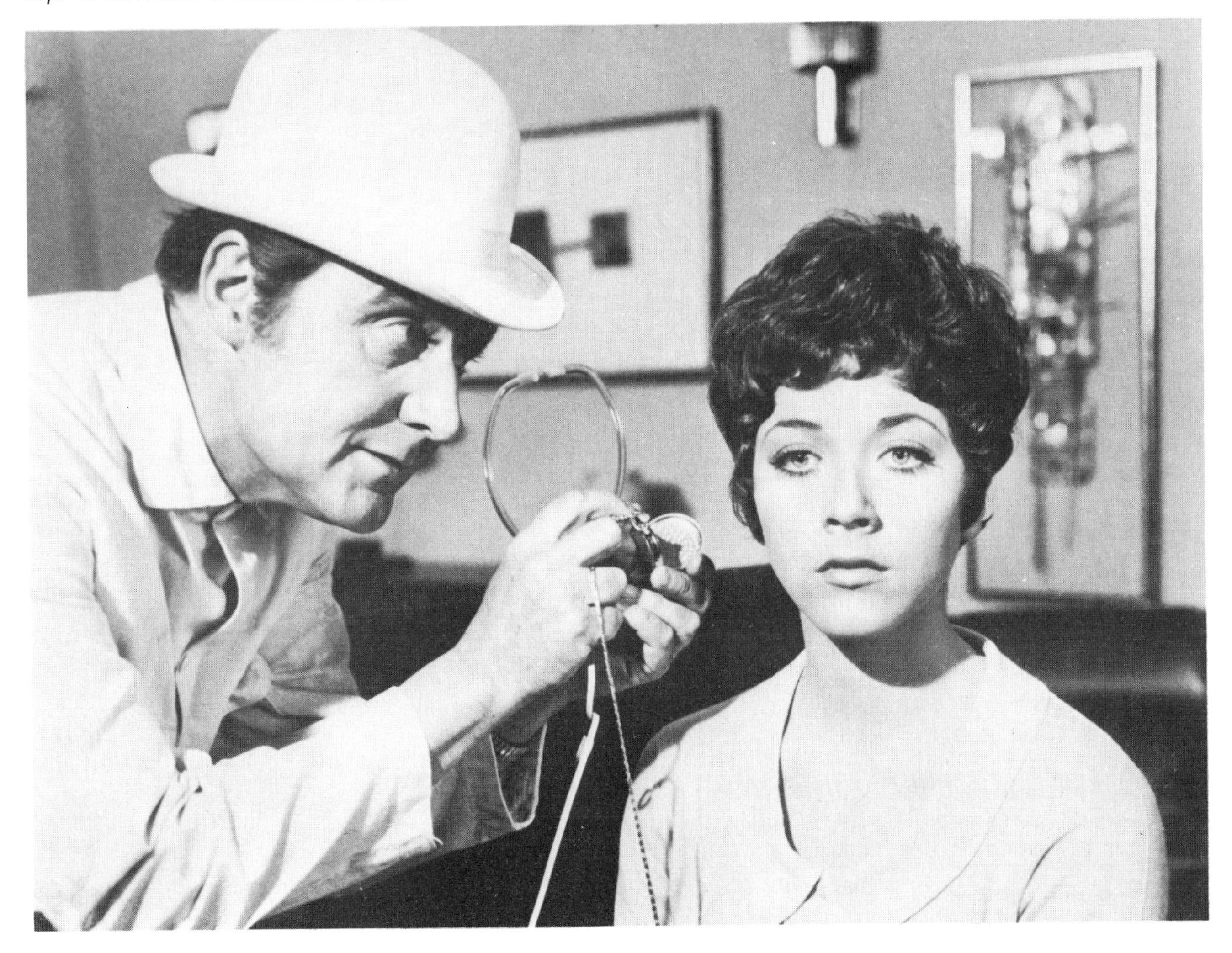

SUBTITLES

Those witty two-line subtitles which followed the main story title in both the Rigg monochrome and colour series (and were written, incidentally, by Brian Clemens) have become as much a trademark of the series as Steed's bowler. However, in subsequent repeats of *The Avengers* many of these have fallen foul of the editor's scissors or have been 'lost' to enable the programme to accommodate a designated time slot. Collected here for the very first time are all fifty subtitles which will test your powers of observation to the full.

Incidentally, though some of the marriages of subtitles to story titles are perfectly obvious, others are not and have been juggled around. Also, to make life more interesting, the supporting photographs are not captioned, giving the eagle-eyed among you the opportunity to identify each photo with its appropriate episode title. A guide to the correct sequence of subtitles, story titles and photographs has been presented on page 118.

1 THE TOWN OF NO RETURN
~ In Which Steed Flies to Nowhere ~
And Emma Does Her Party Piece

2 THE GRAVEDIGGERS
~ In Which Steed Seeks a Wife ~
And Emma Gets Buried

3 THE CYBERNAUTS
~ In Which Steed Receives a Deady Gift ~
And Emma Pockets it

4 DEATH AT BARGAIN PRICES
~ In Which Steed Dabbles in Tycoonery ~
And Emma in Chicanery

5 CASTLE DE'ATH
~ In Which Steed Becomes a Strapping Jock ~
And Emma Lays a Ghost

6 THE MASTER MINDS
~ In Which Steed Joins a Secret Society ~
And Emma Walks the Plank

7 THE MURDER MARKET
In Which Steed Becomes a Gentleman's
~ Gentleman And Emma Faces A Fate ~
Worse Than Death

8 A SURFEIT OF H_2O
~ In Which Steed Makes a Bomb ~
And Emma is Put to Sleep

9 THE HOUR THAT NEVER WAS
~ In Which Steed Becomes a Genius ~
And Emma Loses Her Mind

10 DIAL A DEADLY NUMBER
~ In Which Steed Almost Outbids Himself ~
And Emma is a Bird in a Gilded Cage

11 THE MANEATER OF SURREY GREEN
~ In Which Steed Kills a Climber ~
And Emma Becomes a Vegetable

12 TWO'S A CROWD
~ In Which Steed Goes out of His Mind ~
And Emma is Beside Herself

13 TOO MANY CHRISTMAS TREES
~ In Which Steed Relives a Nightmare ~
And Emma Sees Daylight

14 SILENT DUST
~ In Which Steed Watches Birds ~
And Emma Goes Hunting

15 ROOM WITHOUT A VIEW
~ In Which Steed Takes a Wrong Turning ~
And Emma Holds the Key to All

16 SMALL GAME FOR BIG HUNTERS
~ In Which Steed Fancies Pigeons ~
And Emma Gets the Bird

17 THE GIRL FROM AUNTIE
~ In Which Steed Changes Partners ~
And Emma Joins the Enemy

18 THE 13TH HOLE
~ In Which Steed Finds a Mine of Information ~
And Emma Goes Underground

19 THE QUICK, QUICK SLOW DEATH
~ In Which Steed has Two Left Feet ~
And Emma Dances with Danger

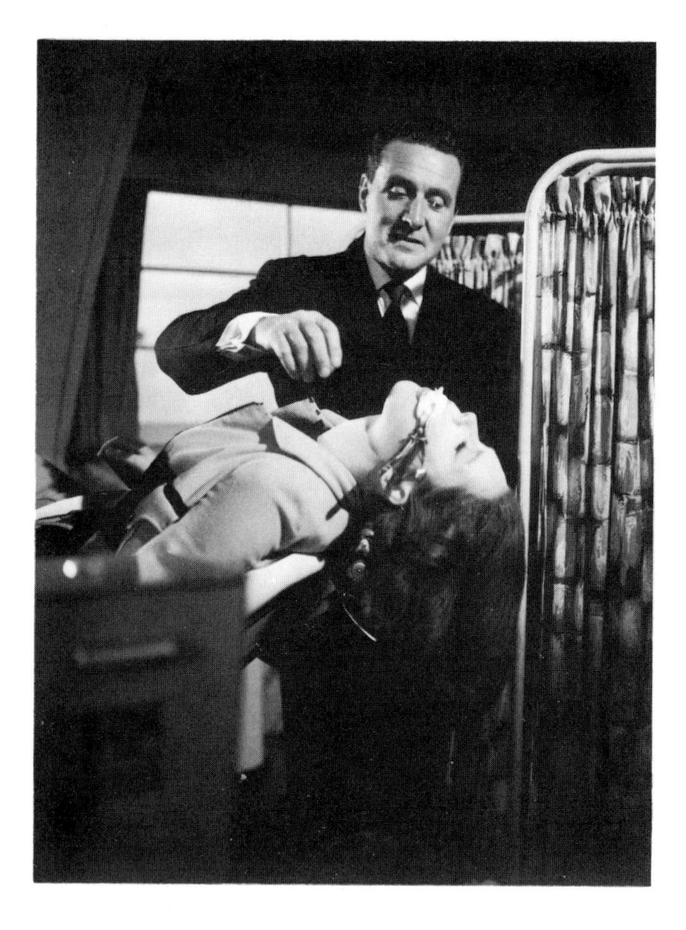

20 THE DANGER MAKERS
~ In Which Steed Makes the Sparks Fly ~
And Emma Gets Switched On

21 A TOUCH OF BRIMSTONE
~ In Which Steed Joins the Hellfire Club ~
And Emma Becomes the Queen of Sin

22 WHAT THE BUTLER SAW
~ In Which Steed Finds a Town Full of Ghosts ~
And Emma Gets Put into Harness

23 THE HOUSE THAT JACK BUILT
~ In Which Steed Dons a Gown ~
And Emma Becomes a Don

24 A SENSE OF HISTORY
~ In Which Steed Goes Bird Watching ~
And Emma does a Comic Strip

25 HOW TO SUCCEED AT MURDER . . .
WITHOUT REALLY TRYING
~ In Which Steed Rallies Around ~
And Emma Drives for Her Life

26 HONEY FOR THE PRINCE
~ In Which Steed Joins the Natives ~
And Emma Gets the Evil Eye

27 FROM VENUS WITH LOVE
~ In Which Steed is Shot Full of Holes ~
And Emma Sees Stars

28 THE FEAR MERCHANTS
~ In Which Steed Becomes a Genie ~
And Emma Joins a Harem

29 ESCAPE IN TIME
~ In Which Steed Becomes a Gourmet ~
And Emma Awakes in Manchuria

30 THE SEE-THROUGH MAN
~ In Which Steed is Single Minded ~
And Emma Sees Double

31 THE BIRD WHO KNEW TOO MUCH
~ In Which Steed Finds a Bogey ~
And Emma Gets a Birdie

32 THE WINGED AVENGER
~ In Which Steed Puts Out a Light ~
And Emma Takes Fright

33 THE LIVING DEAD
~ In Which Steed Meets a Dead Man ~
And Emma Fights the Corpse

34 THE HIDDEN TIGER
~ In Which Steed Hunts a Big Cat ~
And Emma is Badly Scratched

35 THE CORRECT WAY TO KILL
~ In Which Steed Drives a Train ~
And Emma is Tied to the Tracks

36 NEVER, NEVER SAY DIE
~ In Which Steed Hangs Up His Stocking ~
And Emma Asks for More

37 EPIC
~ In Which Steed Catches a Falling Star ~
And Emma Makes a Movie

38 THE SUPERLATIVE SEVEN
~ In Which Steed Trumps an Ace ~
And Emma Plays a Lone Hand

39 **A FUNNY THING HAPPENED ON THE WAY TO THE STATION**
~ In Which Steed Visits the Barber ~
And Emma Has a Close Shave

40 **SOMETHING NASTY IN THE NURSERY**
~ In Which Emma Marries Steed ~
And Steed Becomes a Father

41 **THE JOKER**
~ In Which Steed Plans a Boat Trip ~
And Emma Gets Very Wet

42 **WHO'S WHO**
~ In Which Steed Fights in Ladies' Underwear ~
And Emma Tries 'Feinting'

43 **RETURN OF THE CYBERNAUTS**
~ In Which Steed Pulls Some Strings ~
And Emma Becomes a Puppet

44 **DEATH'S DOOR**
~ In Which Steed Acquires a Nanny ~
And Emma Shops for Toys

45 **THE £50,000 BREAKFAST**
~ In Which Steed Chases a Million ~
And Emma Walks Off with it

46 **DEAD MAN'S TREASURE**
~ In Which Steed Plays Bulls and Bears ~
And Emma Has No Option

47 **YOU HAVE JUST BEEN MURDERED**
~ In Which Steed Becomes a Perfect Boss ~
And Emma Goes Seeking Charm

48 **THE POSITIVE-NEGATIVE MAN**
~ In Which Steed Goes Off the Rails ~
And Emma Finds Her Station in Life

49 **MURDERSVILLE**
~ In Which Steed Has to Face the Music ~
And Emma Disappears

50 **MISSION HIGHLY IMPROBABLE**
~ In Which Steed Falls into Enemy Hands ~
And Emma is Cut Down to Size

MERCHANDISE – A LICENCE TO SELL
A full guide to Avengers/New Avengers spin-offs

One aspect of promoting *The Avengers* both here and abroad was merchandise. The production companies (ABC TV/Thames) earned royalties from the sales of *Avengers* 'tie-ins', and during the Sixties numerous items of related merchandise were licensed. The market was soon saturated with merchandise issued by the biggest and most popular names in the trade. Books, annuals, comic strips, toys, dolls, miniatures of Steed's Bentley and Emma's Lotus, records – aficionados of the series had a field day and quickly found they needed bottomless pockets to keep in step with the amount of merchandise the show had spawned.

Though the following list includes only those items of merchandise known to have been issued and there may be other items I have overlooked, it is the most comprehensive guide ever published and will prove an invaluable asset to the serious collector.

Obviously, with the passage of time, many of the items listed have disappeared or lie 'lost' and forgotten in someone's attic. However, many items do still exist, and a morning spent searching the shelves of your local junk shop or a visit to a nearby jumble sale can unearth many a priceless item.

In each case, I have followed the description with a bracketed figure. This denotes the price you can expect to pay for that item today and is based on my own experiences of the collectors' market. Happy hunting.

THE AVENGERS

Toys and Related Items

The Corgi Gift Set No 40 is perhaps the best known – and certainly the most collectable – of these. Issued in 1966 at a list price of 16/9d (86p), this set contained replicas of Steed's 1929 Bentley and Emma's Lotus Elan.

The Corgi catalogue (complete with reproductions of the two cars plus two miniature photographs of Steed and Emma) described the package in this way: 'Steed's Bentley has been impeccably reproduced right down to the bonnet strap, spiked wheels and detailed interior, with a figure of John Steed at the wheel. Emma's Lotus Elan, complete with standing figure of Emma, is fitted with opening bonnet, plated engine and detailed interior with tip-up seat and suspension. The company actually went so far as to include three moulded plastic umbrellas. The complete set was offered in an attractive presentation box which had artwork of Steed and Emma on both top and sides, and when opened it revealed a display unit with further artwork.

For some inexplicable reason, Corgi insisted on issuing the set with a red (not racing green) Bentley and a white (not powder blue) Lotus, so a word of caution to anyone being offered a set containing a green Bentley: Corgi issued a further Bentley model in 1967, and though this contained a bowler-hatted figure behind the wheel it is in fact based on another television series, *The World of Wooster*, and has no connection with *The Avengers*.

Incidentally, though Corgi relicensed the *Avengers* set in 1969 and planned to issue a further model, no further set was issued owing to the model's dyes being destroyed in a fire at the factory . (£20/24)

The Avengers Jigsaw Puzzles, a set of four, was manufactured by Thomas, Hope & Sankey exclusively for Woolworth's in 1966. Each puzzle consisted of 340 pieces and was 11x17 inches in size.

This highly-prized and much sought after set was based on episodes from the first (Rigg b/w) filmed series. Each contained an artist-depicted scene on both puzzle and box.

The first in the series featured a scene from *Castle De'ath* and depicted Steed, complete with kilt and sword, warding off an attack by a fearsome-looking bearded opponent as he descends down a stone staircase. Emma is featured in the background pinning a second thug to the floor with her foot while holding him at gunpoint.

The second puzzle contains a scene based on *Death at Bargain Prices,* and shows a leather-clad Mrs Peel throwing a villain down a flight of stairs in the basement sports department of a large store. Her colleague stands over a second prostrate figure, brolly at the ready.

The third in the series depicts Steed pinned to a large outdoor archery target by an arrow, while Emma holds the archer at gunpoint. The scene is based on *The Master Minds.*

The final puzzle is, if you'll pardon the pun, a puzzle indeed, and shows Steed and a rather obese gentleman fighting as they

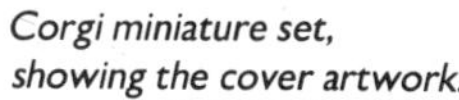

Corgi miniature set, showing the cover artwork.

hang precariously out of an open railway carriage door. Mrs Peel, viewed in the next compartment, holds her opponent in an armlock. Though we are given to believe that this is based on *The Gravediggers*, Mrs Peel's attire (a white beret, complete with 'target' motif) points to this being based on *The Town of No Return* – no such scene appeared in either story! (Each puzzle £5, the set of four £22).

The John Steed Sword Stick was also issued in 1966. Described in the manufacturer's catalogue as 'a plastic toy sword stick, for use also as a water pistol', this is extremely rare. (£3/4).

The same company also issued a miniature Steel bowler hat to complement the above. (£3)

The Emma Peel Doll, which was manufactured in Hong Kong, is another item that is known to have been issued. It is a 10-inch-high plastic doll, dressed in black leather trousers, a short black woollen coat, white roll-neck sweater and black leather boots. The suit was based on the plastic airman's outfit worn by Diana Rigg in *A Surfeit of H^2O and came complete with a white plastic base and a metal strut to support the doll when standing. The figure is shown holding a gun in her right hand. Other outfits are contained in the package. These range from two further pairs of trousers – one of brown leather, the second in dark grey wool; a white plastic tunic; a black plastic coat; a white plastic rainer (trimmed in black); and a pair of black mittens. The box has a clear plastic front and is yellow with the words THE AVENGERS in large print. When the doll is removed from the box, a black silhouette of Steed is depicted on the rear of the packaging. (£10/15)*

Books

Between the years 1963 and 1969, twelve paperback books were issued to tie in with the television transmissions. Each of these contained an original story based on the characters from the series, and are highly sought after by collectors. The twelve titles are listed in chronological order.

The Avengers by Douglas Enefer (Consul Books, 1963). This features the only story to star Steed and Cathy Gale. (£3.50)

Deadline by Patrick Macnee & Peter Leslie (Hodder & Stoughton, 1965). (£4)

Dead Duck by Patrick Macnee & Peter Leslie (Hodder & Stoughton, 1966). (£4)

Both these titles, starring Steed and Mrs Peel, are regarded as the best in the series, and are extremely rare.

Nine other paperbacks, officially listed as *The Avengers* series, were issued between 1967 and 1969. The first four titles were published jointly in both the UK and USA, while the remaining five titles were distributed in the American market only.

The Floating Game (£3)
The Laugh was on Lazarus (£3)
The Passing of Gloria Munday (£3)
Heil Harris (£4)

All four titles by John Garforth (UK: Panther Books and US: Berkley Medallion Books, 1967)

The Afrit Affair (£3.50)
The Drowned Queen (£3.50)
The Gold Bomb (£4)

All three titles by Keith Laumer (Berkley Medallion Books, 1968).

The Magnetic Man (£3.50)
Moon Express (£3.50)

Both by Norman Daniels (Berkley Medallion Books, 1968 and 1969).

An interesting point is that though Berkley Medallion issued only nine titles, they did in fact license twelve. Four titles were also issued in France, and these are the same as the UK Panther Book titles.

Annuals

The first comic annual to feature The Avengers was published in 1962. Entitled **TV Crimebusters** (TV Productions), this is of particular interest to aficionados of the series as it is the only publication to feature a story starring the original team of John Steed and Dr David Keel. The *Avengers* story, a seven-page story called *The Drug Pedlar,* is of added interest as the strip includes eight stills from the 1961 series and the strip depicts Steed's style of dress during that period. (£7/8)

1967 saw the publication of the first 'official' *Avengers* annuals. Titled, naturally enough, **The Avengers** (Souvenir Press/ Atlas Publications), this contains 92 pages of picture strips and text stories plus various features on the series with Steed and Mrs Peel. The cover depicts Steed and Emma battling it out with two uniformed (Russian?) soldiers on a castle staircase. Also included are 40 b/w and colour photographs. (£6/7) Incidentally, during my research I have discovered references to a second Steed and Emma Peel annual. However, this was not an official publication and was 'bootlegged' by a group of American fans and circulated from their home base in 1966.

The second annual, and the first to feature Tara King, was published in 1968. This contains 80 pages and the cover features a head-and-shoulders shot of Steed wearing a dark suit while sporting the proverbial bowler, brolly and red carnation, plus two smaller drawings of Tara. The annual includes 25 b/w and colour photographs. (£6)

A third annual was issued in 1969, again featuring Steed and Tara, and contains the same number of pages as the previous year's annual. The cover depicts a full-face shot of Steed while Tara, gun at the ready, peers over his left shoulder. This contains 80 pages and 27 b/w and colour photos. (£6)

Other notable publications include: **Meet the Avengers** Star Special 15 (World Distributors, 1963) Advertised as 'an exciting behind-the-scenes visit with the stars of ABC's Top TV Show', this contains 44 pages of text features on the Patrick Macnee/Honor Blackman series. Also included are interviews with both the stars and production staff, and the publication is rounded off with over 30 b/w photographs. This is probably the rarest of all the publications and has appeared on dealers' lists at an incredible £12. A more realistic price is £8.

Comics

The Avengers also featured in numerous comic strip publications. The most notable of these were the stories printed in full colour in **Diana** (1967). Lasting for a period of 26 weeks, this two-page strip pitted Steed and Mrs Peel against such adversaries as: Madame Zingara, a woman who had discovered a method of weaving a trance-inducing material which, when woven into a dress for Mrs Peel, turns Steed's colleague into a mindless zombie; modern-day Vikings loose on the streets of London; Black Heart and her deadly band of midgets; a power-crazed scientist bent on destroying England by the use of 'brainwashed' pet animals; The Mad Hatter, where Steed's

Avengers Annual, 1968

Avengers Annual, 1969

bowler becomes a deadly weapon; and the Sinister Six, a group of six notorious criminals who are bent on destroying The Avengers.

The artwork on this strip was of the highest quality throughout and is a pure delight, making this set a highly-prized and eagerly sought after item. Per single comic (£1), the complete set (£30)

Other comic strip titles include **The Avengers No 1** (Thorpe & Porter, 1966). Published for the UK market, this 68-page, all b/w comic contained four picture strips: *The Mochocks, The K Stands for Killers, No Jury – No Justice* and *Deadly Efficient.* All four stories feature Steed and Mrs Peel. (£3).

John Steed - Emma Peel (Gold Key, 1968). This one-shot, 32-page, all-colour comic was published in the USA and contained two picture stories, *The Roman Invasion* and *The Mirage Maker.* Although the cover title is as above, the comic was actually registered as **The Avengers No 1?** Odder still, the two comic stories were sub-licensed from a UK comic company, Polystyle, which published their own weekly childrens comic. (£2.50)

TV Comic (Polystyle) regularly used an *Avengers* comic strip between 1965 and 1971. The first *Avengers* story appeared in issue no 720 (2 October 1965) and strips featuring Steed and Mrs Peel (and later Tara King) continued to appear on a semi-regular basis until the early Seventies. *Avengers* strips and text stories also appeared in the company's TV Comic annuals. Per comic (15p), per annual (60p)

Further adventures of Steed, Mrs Peel and Tara King could also be found in the London Express Features syndicated comic strip and as Der Wreckers in Germany.

In 1969, the popular UK television journal *TVTimes* published **The TVTimes Diana Rigg Spectacular** – an 8-page all-colour magazine special devoted entirely to Diana Rigg. Features included 'Diana Rigg on Stage', and the centre-page spread pulled out into a giant size 'bioscope' of Diana's career. 18 b/w and colour photographs. Extremely rare, this would probably cost around £4.50 if bought today.

Seven years later, the same company produced a **TVTimes Souvenir Extra – The New Avengers** (1976). Published to coincide with the arrival of *The New Avengers* on our screens, this contained hundreds of photographs and 'Patrick Macnee's Life Story'. (£5/6)

Finally, though not really an *Avengers* item, worthy of note is **Honor Blackman's Book of Self Defence** (Andre Deutsch, 1965).

The introduction is written by Honor herself and contains references to *The Avengers* and the 'Cathy Gale' connection. The book contains over 130 b/w photographs of Honor Blackman being put through a catalogue of judo routines by Black Belt judo expert Joe Robinson, and is well worth keeping an eye open for. (£7).

Records

High on the aficionados' 'most wanted ' memorabilia list are records containing the original (or cover) versions of 'The Avengers Theme' or incidental music pertaining to the programme. However, as the majority of these have long since been deleted, and the chances of finding playable (i.e. unscratched) copies are highly remote, I have refrained from offering a current price guide and simply catalogued the records in their chronological order of release.

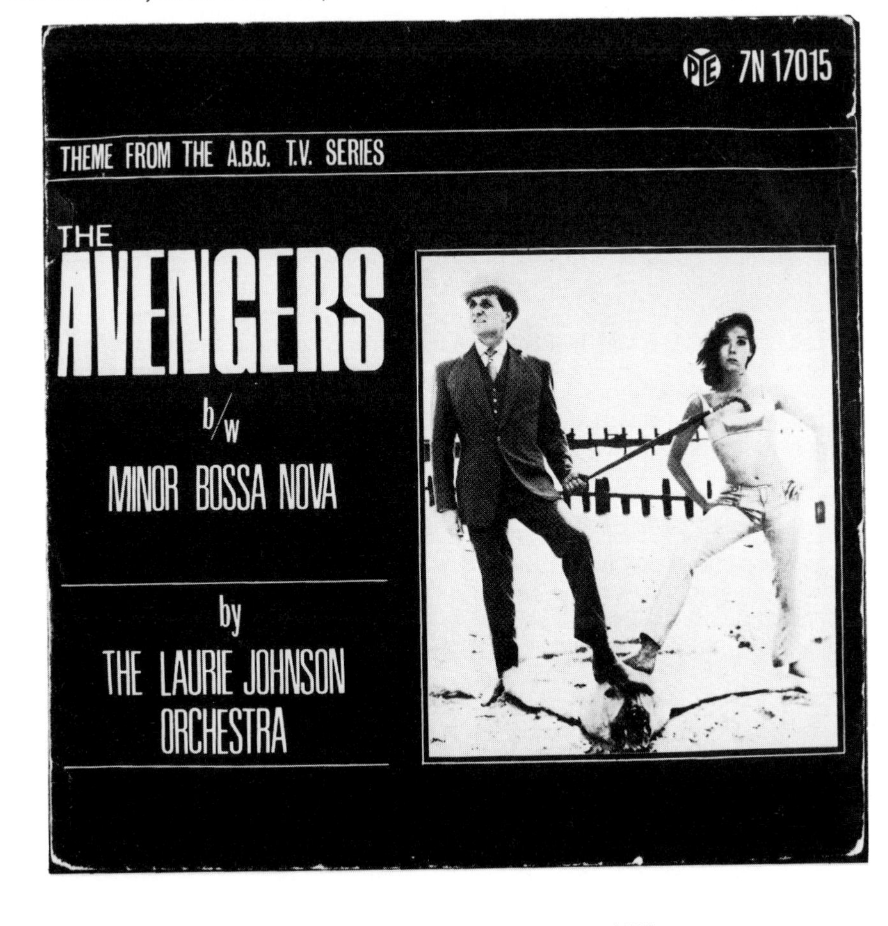

The original sleeve for The Avengers *by the Laurie Johnson Orchestra, 1965.*

Singles

The Avengers by Johnny Dankworth & His Orchestra. Fontana TF422, 1963
Kinky Boots by Patrick Macnee and Honor Blackman. Decca F11843, 1964
The Avengers by The Laurie Johnson Orchestra. Pye TN17015, 1965
TV Themes (featuring the Johnson original theme). Pye NEP 24244 (extended play), 1966
The Avengers by The Joss Loss Orchestra. HMV/POP 1500, 1966
TV Themes – A Gift From Pascal Murray (A special 'give-away' containing the original Johnson theme). MCPS ATV1 (Extended play), 1969
Kinky Boots by Patrick Macnee and Honor Blackman (a 'maxi-single' reissue of the 1964 release. This also contains a cover version of 'The Avengers Theme ' by Roland Shaw). 12 Cherry 62, 1983

Albums

The Avengers and Other TV Themes by The Johnny Gregory Orchestra (Contains a cover version of the Dankworth 'Avengers Theme'). Wing WL1087, 1961
Themes for Secret Agents by The Roland Shaw Orchestra (Contains a cover version of the Johnson 'Avengers Theme'). Decca PFS 4094, 1966
The Avengers Theme and Other TV Music (Contains the original Johnson theme). Hanna Barbara, 1966
The Laurie Johnson Orchestra Plays 'The Avengers'. Marble Arch MAL695, 1967
Time for TV by The Brian Fahey Orchestra (Contains a cover version of the Johnson theme). Studio Two/EMI Two175, 1969
Theme from the Avengers by Jerry Monats Harmonicats (Contains a cover version of the Johnson theme). Hallmark CHM629, 1969
Themes and ... by The Laurie Johnson Orchestra (Contains the original Johnson 'Tara King' Theme, plus the 'Tag Theme' music). MGM/CS 8104, 1969
The Phase 4 World of Thrillers (A compilation album containing the Roland Shaw version). Decca SPA160, 1971
50 Popular TV Themes by The Bruce Baxter Orchestra (A double album, containing a cover version of the Johnson theme). Pickwick 50/DA315, 1977
Music from the Avengers/The New Avengers & The Professionals by The Laurie Johnson Orchestra (Contains selected incidental music from all three series, plus the title theme music. These are not the original dubs, but newly recorded.) UK: Unicorn-Kanchana PRM7009, 1980; US: Starlog/Varese Sarabande ASV/95003

Although the contents were the same in both the UK and USA, the cover wasn't. The UK sleeve opened out into a double sleeve and contained numerous photographs from the series. The US version was issued in a single sleeve which portrayed Steed and Emma framed by a a pair of scales.

Miscellaneous

During the mid Seventies, Derann Film Services, a Midland-based home movie supplier, issued four *Avengers* titles for the home movie market. The episodes were supplied on Super-8mm film and were: *From Venus With Love, The Living Dead, The Positive-Negative Man* and *Return of the Cybernauts.* Each was issued in two formats: a full version on 3 x 400ft reels, and a 15-minute 'condensed' version on 1 x 400ft reel. Sadly, these prints have now been discontinued, prior to which they were offered at a 'bargain' price of £54.95 per 45-minute episode. To achieve the 45-minute length, Derann edited out the opening and closing 'teaser' scenes. The result was most acceptable, and copies of these prints are now being offered at upwards of £60.

A Company called Centaur Films also produced a full-length print of *The £50,000 Breakfast* for the home movie market. This six-reel colour print also had optical sound.

Perhaps not so widely known is that the production company (EMI) licensed six Super-8mm titles to an American company, Sundstand, which supplied many of the world's airlines with in-flight movies. The titles, issued between 1975 and 1978, were: *From Venus With Love, Escape in Time, The Bird Who Knew Too Much, Something Nasty in the Nursery, The £50,000 Breakfast* and *The Positive-Negative Man.* They were then supplied to the French airlines UTA and Air Afrique and were issued in dual language prints so that passengers could listen to the original soundtrack or a French over-dub. This contract expired in 1980, and all six prints were destroyed.

Special merchandising rights were also given to various other outlets.

In 1969, Spillers, the producers of a world-famous brand of pet food, ran a consumer-orientated promotion campaign using *The Avengers* to promote their product. The campaign took the form of a detective/spy story of approximately 1,000 words, and entrants were invited to selected certain salient points in the story that related to the questions asked on the entry form. Over 6½ million packs were distributed to major stores throughout the UK.

In Germany, two major fashion houses joined forces to promote a man-made fashion tie-up. The companies, ICI and Povel, went on to issue both men's and women's wear in the 'new' material. Also in Germany, an enterprising West German umbrella manufacturer, Knirps, used Patrick Macnees's Steed character to promote his new line. He made two TV commercials, and specially selected *Avengers* film clips were used.

Never slow to realise that related merchandise was a money-earner (the production company earned royalties on all items sold), the copyright owners held their own fashion display at a well-known London hotel in 1967. The event, devised and co-ordinated by Edser Southey Design Associates and produced by Michael Edser, promoted over 54 'Avengerwear 67' items. Among these were the entire range of 'Emmapeelers' (the catsuits worn by Diana Rigg in the series), and a range of Pierre Cardin 'Steed' attire, plus shoes, hats, gloves, scarves and bags, etc. Of particular interest to *Avengers* buffs was the special entrance 'ticket' supplied for the occasion. This took the form of a standard-size playing card and featured a joint image of Mrs Peel and Steed as the Queen and Knave of Hearts. 'Steed' shirts in Bri-nylon, styled in Saville Row and complete with bowler and brolly motif; a cheque-book-shaped catalogue from John Temple Tailoring, including Patrick Macnee complete with dolly bird (and gun?); Avengers wrist watches – two models, The Avenger at £4.19s.6d and The Great Avenger at £5.10s – the list is endless. Sadly, most of these items are now lost or destroyed, or in the case of dresswear, worn out and discarded.

One of the items licensed though never issued would have been high on the list of collectables by aficionados. This was a set of two separate bubble-gum cards, containing over 144 colour photographs (one set each for Patrick/Diana, Patrick/Linda). These were licensed by a West German sweets and confectionery company in 1970 to tie-in with the German television screenings.

Reproduction of the entry ticket for the fashion show held in 1967.

THE NEW AVENGERS

Toys and Related Items

Like its predecessor, the *New Avengers* production company cast its eyes towards the merchandise market and numerous items of interest were issued.

Dinky Toys issued two die-cast model cars in 1977. The first of these, Model No 112 **Purdey's TR7,** was, according to *The Dinky Toy Price Guide* (Ernest Benn, 1982), issued in two different formats. One has silver flashes on its doors and sides, with black and silver trim with white interior. A black letter 'P' is on the bonnet and the model was designed with a double 'V' in silver in front of it. The second model is green in colour, and has the full word Purdey on the bonnet. The second model is worth more. (£10/15)

The second model, No 113 **Steed's Special Leyland Jaguar,** was advertised in the Dinky catalogue, but was never officially issued – although several prototype models were illegally 'spirited-out' of the factory and are therefore very rare and worth a great deal of money. In medium green, greenish blue or medium blue with gold stripes along each side, the model is also know to exist with a long orange flash, silver wheels and bumpers. With white or fawn interior and a figure of 'Steed' at the wheel. (£40/50)

A similar fate – that of being stolen from the factory – befell Model No 307 **The New Avengers Gift Set.** Never officially released, this contained Purdey's TR7 and Steed's Special Leyland Jaguar, plus a novel fly-off assailant. Price today ... £100!

At the lower end of the price scale – though still highly collectable – are two **Revell Plastic Assembly Kits: Purdey's TR7** and **Gambit's XJS** (1979). The first, issued in yellow and black plastic, and the second, in red and black, were both 1:25 scale models and came in easy-to-assemble kit form and nicely produced boxes with photos of Purdey and Gambit on each (£6)

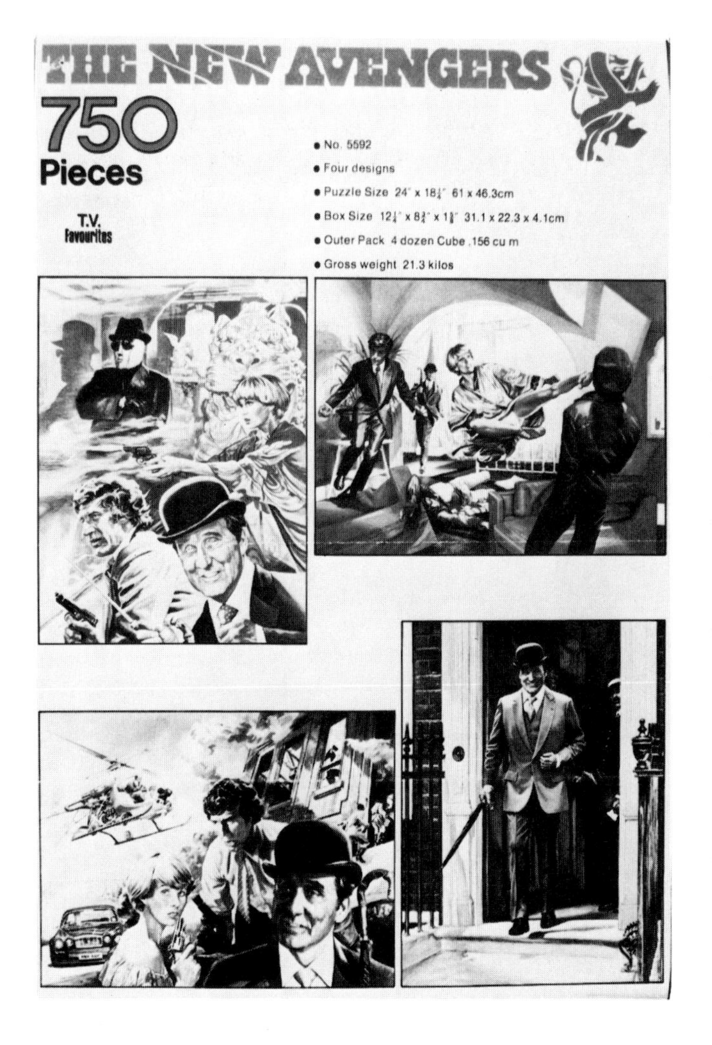

The New Avengers also spawned some children's games. Of these, **The New Avengers Mission Kit** (Thomas Salter, 1976) is the most collectable. This was issued with a photograph of the trio on the lid and contains a plastic gun and silencer, plastic holster, hand-grenade, magnifying glass and an assortment of cardboard cut-outs that in turn make up a 'code breaker'. Also included are a paper passport and, or so the manufacturer would have us believe, a plastic camera that actually works. Originally retailed at £4.95, the kit is now worth £8.

'An exciting game for 2-4 players' is the way **The New Avengers Board Game** (Denys Fisher, 1977) was described. The game comes complete with a nicely designed board, a bowler hat and umbrella spinner, plus playing models. In fact the game is as 'exciting' as Ludo. (£5)

There is also **The New Avengers Shooting Game** (Denys Fisher, 1976). Intended for 2-4 players, this comes in an attractive presentation box and contains cardboard cut-out figures, a clockwork-operated window set in a cardboard cut-out house and the object of the game (based no doubt on the story *'Target')* is to shoot cardboard silhouettes out of the windows, provided the enclosed guns and pellets work – mine seldom do! (£6)

Arrow Games issued a set of four **New Avengers Jigsaw Puzzles** in 1976. Each measures 24 by 18¼ inches and comes complete with artist-depicted designs. The first of these has Steed, Purdey and Gambit in the foreground against an action backcloth of a car, helicopter and burning buildings. The second puzzle portrays Purdey giving an action-packed kick to Kane's Cybernaut, while Steed and Gambit race to her rescue. Puzzle three displays a montage of the New Avengers and a Cybernaut, and the final puzzle depicts Steed leaving Number 10, Downing Street. Bearing in mind that these had a cover price of £1.10 each, one can expect to pay £5 today.

Female fans of the series could also buy the official **Purdey Doll,** though I suspect that many males were also tempted to do so. Manufactured by Denys Fisher, the figure was dressed in the purple leotard worn by Joanna Lumley in *The Eagle's Nest,* complete with tights, shoes and a patterned skirt. Further outfits were advertised on the back of the package. In the words of the manufacturer, 'Purdey leads such an exciting life, she needs an outfit for every occasion.' For special dates, there was a cream trouser suit with chiffon trimmings; for glamorous occasions, an elegant black dress with fur stole or a green halter-neck dress with long flowing scarf; for relaxing, a rust-coloured jump-suit or a red catsuit; and for practical wear, a suede trouser suit with matching hat and scarf. The 10-inch-high doll was sealed in a plastic bubble on a cardboard display board, which had an artist-depicted drawing of Joanna Lumley on the cover (£6/7)

Books

Only six *New Avengers* paperbacks were issued during the course of the series and, unlike the *Avengers* books which contained original stories based on the characters, the *New Avengers* books were novelisations based on selected episodes from the series. All six titles were published by Futura Books and, in chronological order, were:

House of Cards by Peter Cave 1976 (£2)
The Eagle's Nest by John Carter 1976 (£2)
To Catch a Rat by Walter Harris 1976 (£2)
Fighting Men by Justin Cartright 1977 (£3)
The Cybernauts by Peter Cave 1977 (£3)
Hostage by Peter Cave 1977 (£3)

The last three titles were not published in the USA, so these are marginally more valuable for collectors.

One other notable publication is **John Steed – An Authorised Biography,** Vol 1, 'Jealous in Honour' by Tim Heald (Weidenfeld & Nicolson, 1977). This contained a fictionalised account of Steed's childhood and early career, and though well-written and interesting – particularly a chapter in which Steed dumps the college bully (a certain James Bond) on his backside – the book fails to give any account of Steed's earlier undercover activities and ends with his first meeting with Cathy Gale. Though the book was meant to be the first in a series, disappointing sales stopped further editions beings issued. (£6/7)

Annuals

In 1977, Brown and Watson published the first of two *New Avengers* annuals. This contained 64 pages of text and picture stories, and was complemented by over 40 b/w and colour photographs. The second annual was issued a year later, and followed the same format but this time contained over 50 photographs. Each annual sells for £5 in today's market.

For the *Avengers* completist, the same company produced a 1979 annual called **TV Detectives,** which contained two pages on Gambit and Purdey. (£2)

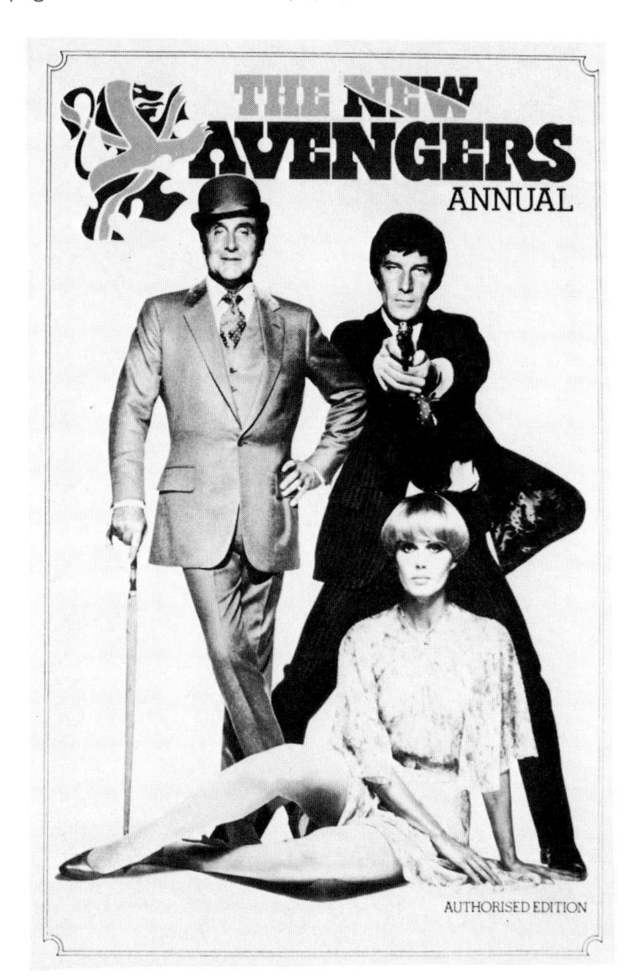

Records

Only two singles were released between 1976 and 1980. The first of these, **The New Avengers Theme** by The Laurie Johnson Orchestra, EMI 2562, was a faithful version of the *New Avengers* theme, and contained an added bonus in the form of 'A Flavour of *The New Avengers'* on side two. This gave extracts from a couple of the episodes, complete with a car-chase in stereo. Another plus factor was that the single was issued in a full-colour picture sleeve.

It was 1980 before a second 'official' version of the *New Avengers* theme was issued. Once again in a picture sleeve, this contained **The New Avengers Main Title Theme,** played by the London Studio Orchestra, conducted by Laurie Johnson, and is a single version of the same track from The Avengers/ The New Avengers/The Professionals album mentioned earlier. Unicorn-Kanchana C15.

To my knowledge, only one album was released during this period. This was issued by Reader's Digest and contained a new recording of the *New Avengers* theme played by The London Festival Orchestra, conducted by Burt Rhodes.

Miscellaneous

Other notable *New Avengers* items include a rub-down set of transfers from Letraset (1977). This contains a scene from the episode *Last of the Cybernauts...?* and depicts Kane and his metal-headed sidekicks in pursuit of Steed, Purdey and Gambit. (£1.50)

Scandecor Posters issued a giant-size poster of the trio in 1976, but this was quickly sold out. No replacement poster was ever issued.

Fashionwise, very little (if anything?) was offered during the series' lifespan, though Joanna Lumley did model for a window-display mannequin and her face could be seen in dozens of women's fashion-house windows. Then, of course, Patrick Macnee endorsed 'Right Guard' body deodorant, Colibri lighter products and made two television ads for Vauxhall motors.

Fan Magazines

Although I have already covered the professional magazines available, one aspect of published merchandise that certainly warrants a mention here is Fanzines – which perhaps I should define. As the name implies, the word was coined by collectors to describe a fan magazine – a publication produced by fans for fans. These can range from the simple quality of the 'home-grown' product (usually produced on a duplicating machine) to the more professional (and expensive) typeset product. In some cases, magazines are produced by over-zealous fans who, though their intentions are sincere, often cannot afford to maintain the finance needed and these magazines seldom survive two or three issues.

Strange though it may appear, despite its enormous popularity *The Avengers* never received as much fanzine coverage as other popular shows of the period. However, one or two magazines were issued during its lifespan, and of these a few are worthy of mention. Probably the best of those issued during the Sixties was one produced in the USA called **En Garde.** It was produced quarterly and ran to eight issues, with numbers 1 to 4, 5 and 6 being of particular interest to fans of the show. A second well-produced American magazine was **The Avengers/Patrick Macnee Fan Newsletter.** Produced between 1978 and 1980 by young *Avengers* enthusiast Heather Firth, each issue came complete with photographs, interviews and interesting text features on the stars.

One year later, a UK fan club, **The Avengers Appreciation Society,** produced two fanzines based on the show (June/Autumn 1981). The first was an 8-page introductory issue, while the second contained 20 pages of features and photographs.

In April 1982, David Caruba, hooked on the series when it first began syndication in the USA during the early Seventies, issued the first photocopied edition of **With Umbrella, Charm and Bowler** (being the American translation of the German name for *The Avengers* – 'Mit Schirm, Charme and Melone') and this was followed four months later by issue 2. By January 1983 the magazine had proved so popular that the publication was continued in a professionaly-printed newspaper format, and the fanzine increased in both circulation and page count (latest issue 20 pages) until today each issue is avidly awaited by *Avengers* fans throughout the world.

Last but not least (in my opinion!) of the current *Avengers* magazines is my own fanzine offering, **On Target – The Avengers.** Now entering its third year of publication, the magazine is published four times yearly and each issue contains a minimum of 20 pages of 'rare' photographs plus interesting and thought-provoking articles. Anyone wishing to obtain further information should drop a line to the *OT* editorial address: 114 Dartmouth Street, Burslem, Stoke-on-Trent, Staffs. ST6 1HE.

Part of the card display board that came complete with the 'Purdey' doll – showing the range of outfits.

THE AVENGERS' CAST LIST

In view of the immense popularity of *The Avengers,* it is hardly surprising that in its heyday many of today's world-famous names – then, of course, mainly supporting players – deigned to appear in the series. In fact, during the Sixties it soon became the 'in' programme on which to be seen, and many performers actually asked their agents to book them for an appearance!

The show had a cast of thousands – names which, if required today, would elevate the production cost to the million-dollar bracket. For example, take two young people who had barely started their acting careers and appeared together in one episode. Their names: Donald Sutherland (today one of the cinema's biggest money-earners) and Charlotte Rampling (now one of Hollywood's favourite female stars). Imagine paying for their joint talents today!

Screen protagonists Peter Cushing and Christopher Lee appeared on four occasions in the series – though never at the same time. The comedy talents of John Cleese, Ronnie Barker and Jon Pertwee brought madcap humour to the series. Also in the role of honour are Penelope Keith and Peter Bowles, stars of the *To the Manor Born.* And long before they donned the personae of Bodie and Doyle of *The Professionals,* Lewis Collins and Martin Shaw worked as a team in *The Avengers* – albeit on the side of the villains.

Look through the following list of names and see how many of today's celebrities appeared as guest stars or played cameo roles during the lifetime of *The Avengers.*

Frederick Abbott
Joss Ackland
Ronald Adam
Tom Adams
Tony Adams
Raymond Adamson
Anthony Ainley
Geoffrey Alexander
Terence Alexander
Patrick Allen
Ronald Allen
Wendy Allnutt
Jacky Allouis
Nicholas Amer
Iann Anders
Daphne Anderson
David Anderson
Esther Anderson
Keith Anderson
Maria Andipa
Annette Andre
Margo Andrew
David Andrews
Paul Anil
Philip Anthony

Edwin Apps
Bernard Archard
Nigel Arkright
Graham Armitage
Julia Arnall
Peter Arne
Grace Arnold
Harvey Ashby
Graham Ashley
Coral Atkins
John Attkinson
Katy Attwood
Liane Aukin
Ray Austin

Robert G Bahey
John Bailey
Redmond Bailey
Anthony Baird
John Baker
Mark Baker
Michael Balfour
Ralph Ball
Freda Bamford

Trevor Bannister
John Barcroft
Gillian Barday
Eric Barker
Ronnie Barker
Peter Barkworth
Bruce Barnabe
Patrick Barr
John Barrard
Arthur Barratt
Ray Barratt
Reginald Barratt
Tim Barratt
June Barrett
Frank Barringer
David Barron
John Barron
Keith Barron
Anthony Bate
Timothy Bateson
David Bauer
Beryl Baxter
Keith Baxter
Geoffrey Bayldon
Peter Bayliss

Richard Beddo
Michael Beint
Ann Bell
Valerie Bell
James Bellchamber
Len Belmont
Kenneth Bender
Christopher Benjamin
John Bennett
George Benson
Hamlyn Benson
Harold Berens
Dawn Beret
Robert Bernal
Kevin Berry
Carole Beyer
Sylvia Bidmead
Charles Bird
David Bird
Norman Bird
Penny Bird
Cynthia Bizeray
Isobel Black
Anthony Blackshaw
Douglas Blackwell

Isla Blair
Katherine Blake
Colin Blakeley
Alan Blakelock
Caroline Blakiston
Brian Blessed
Newton Blick
John Bluthal
Peter Blythe
Michael Bolton
Bruce Boa
Gary Bond
Philip Bond
Anthony Booth
Roger Booth
Peter Bourne
Lally Bowers
Norman Bowler
Peter Bowles
Gordon Boyd
Wilfred Boyle
Irene Bradshaw
Brandon Brady
Terence Brady
Edward Brayshaw

James Bree
Kevin Brennan
Terry Brewer
Tony Van Bridge
Tim Brinton
Peter Bromdow
Lyndon Brook
Ray Brookes
A J Brown
Bernard Brown
Edwin Brown
Ray Brown
Robert Brown
Angela Browne
Alan Browning
Michael Browning
Graham Bruce
Judy Bruce
Robert Bruce
Kathleen Bryon
William Buck
Denise Buckley
Keith Buckley
Hugh Burden
Alfred Burke
Jonathan Burn
Edward Burnham
Jeremy Burnham
Larry Burns
Lionel Burns
Sheila Burrell
Peter Burton
Richard Butler
Janet Butlin

Edward Caddick
John Cairney
Richard Caldicott
Joyce Carey
David Cargill
Patrick Cargill
John Carlisle
Charles Carson
Meron Carvic
Alan Casley
Susan Castle
John Cater
Pearl Catlin
Tony Caunter
Dallas Cavell
Robert Cawdron
John Cazabon
John Chados
Julia Chagrin
Naomi Chance
Constance Chapman
Norman Chappell
Vincent Charles
Geoffrey Chater
Cecil Cheng
Alan Chintz
Christopher Chittell
Joyce Wong Chong
Jennifer Chulow
Denise Chunnery
John Church
Diane Clare
Ian Clarke
Richard Clarke
Warren Clarke
Peter Clay
Virginia Clay
Denise Cleary
John Cleese
Carol Cleveland
John Cobner
Michael Coccoran
Emma Cochrane
John Coidey
Noel Coleman
Richard Coleman
Sylvia Coleridge
Michael Coles
Ian Colin
Clive Colin-Bowler
Christopher Coll
Kenneth Colley
Patience Collier
Michael Collins
Geoffrey Colville
Nigel Colville
John Comer
Miranda Connell
Edric Connor
Patrick Connor
Jan Conrad
Pamela Conway
George A Cooper
Kenneth Cope
James Copeland
Peter Copley
Delia Corrio
James Cossins
Nicholas Courtney
Roger Cowdren
Breda Cowling
Arthur Cox
Clifford Cox
Gerry Crampton
Les Crawford
Bernard Cribbins
John Crocker
Gerald Cross
Hugh Cross
Larry Cross
Jennifer Croxton
Ronald Culver
Douglas Cummings
Bill Cummins
Anthony Cundell
Anna Cunningham
Ian Cunningham
Margo Cunningham
Richard Curnock
Annette Currall
Roland Curram
Ian Curry
John Curson
Alan Curtis
Lucinda Curtis
Peter Cushing
Allan Cuthbertson
Iain Cuthbertson
Jonathan Cuttney

Joanne Dainton
Andre Dakar
Paul Dakins
Amy Dalby
Paul Danguah
Bandana Das Gupta
Nigel Davenport
Michael David
David Davies
Griffith Davies
Alexander Davion
Noel Davis
Pamela Ann Davy
Anthony Dawes
Paul Dawkins
Carmen Dean
Ivor Dean
Robert Dean
John Dearth
Felix Deebank
Guy Deghby
Aimee Delamain
Pauline Delaney
Roger Delgado
Zulena Dene
Rosemary Denham
Peter Dennis
Jay Denver
Patricia Denys
Robert Desmond
William Devlin
Arnold Diamond
Peter Diamond
Cliff Diggens
Basil Dingham
Vernon Dobtcheff
Eric Dodson
Guy Doleman
Donel Donnelly
James Donnelly
Rosemary Donnelly
Sandra Drone
Angela Douglas
Donald Douglas
Fabia Drake
Gabrielle Drake
Moira Drummond
Vivianne Drummond
Carl Duering
Philip Dunbar
Clive Dunn
Ruth Dunning
Storm Durr
Anthony Dutton
Valentine Dyall
Hamilton Dyce
Leon Eagles
Clifford Earl
Donald Eccles
Paul Eddington
Mark Eden
Dennis Edwards
Glyn Edwards
Sandor Eles
Clifford Elkin
Terry Eliot
Eric Elliot
Peter Elliot
Peter J Elliott
Colin Ellis
William Ellis
Catharine Ellison
Jonathan Elsom
Mark Elwes
Patricia English
Hetti Erich
Clifford Evans
Tenniel Evans

Michael Faire
Frederick Fairley
John Falconer
James Falkland
Rio Fanning
Derek Farr
Charles Farrell
Kenneth Farrington
Truder Faulkner
Sheila Fearn
Sandra Fehr
Christine Ferdinando
Fred Ferris
Fenella Fielding
Lucy Fleming
Robert Flemying
John Flint
Eric Flynn
Peter Fontaine
Scott Forbes
Karen Ford
Michael Forrest
Denis Forsyth
Dudley Foster
Edward Fox
William Fox
John Fraidey
Susan Franklin
William Franklyn
Alice Fraser
Bill Fraser
Ronald Fraser
Liz Frazer
Leslie French
Martin Friend
Tex Fuller
Lynne Furlong

Liam Gaffney
Gordon Gardner
John Garrie
David Garth
Frank Gatliff
William Gaunt
Eunice Gayson
Donald Gee
Archilles Gorgion
George Ghent
Philip Gilbert
John Gill
Tom Gill
Paul Gillard
Robert Gillespie
Tony Gilpin
Leslie Galzer
David Glover
Julian Glover
John Glyn-Johns
Willoughby Goddard
George Goderick
Anne Godfrey
Derek Godfrey
Tommy Godfrey
Anne Godley
Michael Goldie
Bernard Goldman
Maurice Good
Michael Goodliffe
Lyndhall Goodman
Harold Goodwin
Howard Goorney
James Gori
Michael Gough
Hazel Graeme
Clive Graham
Willoughby Gray
Richard Graydon
Nigel Green
Leon Greene
John Greenwood
Katy Greenwood
Joseph Greig
David Gregory
Rowena Gregory
Janine Grey
Stephan Gryff
Arthur Griffiths
Jack Grossman
Wilfred Grove
Philip Guard
Mal Gulili
Sheila Gummons
John Gurrie
John Gutrell
Jack Gwillim
Michael Gwynn

Ingrid Hafner
Fred Haggerty
Harvey Hail
Brian Haines
Patricia Haines
Neil Hallet
Noel Hallett

Peter Halliday
Ian Hamilton
Roger Hammond
Stephen Hancock
Paul Hansard
Vincent Harding
Paul Hardwick
Laurence Hardy
Doris Hare
Janet Hargreaves
Juliet Harmer
Gerald Harper
Robert Harris
David Hart
Louis Haslar
Imogen Hassall
Brian Hawkins
Michael Hawkins
James Hayter
Alan Haywood
Maurice Hedley
John G Heller
Drewe Henley
Joyce Heron
Arthur Hewlett
Edward Higgins
Ronald Hines
Andy Ho
Raymond Hodge
Charles Hogson
Jan Holden
John Hollis
Patrick Holt
Ewan Hooper
Gary Hope
Penelope Horner
Walter Horsburgh
Bernard Horsfall
John Horsley
Basil Hoskins
Charles Houston
Arthur Howard
Ken Howard
Arthur Howell
Peter Howell
Walter Hudd
Vanda Hudson
Neville Hughes
Peter Hughes
Lloyd Humble
Michael Hunt
Alistair Hunter
John Hussey
Murray Hutchinson
Ross Hutchinson
Ric Hutton

Barrie Ingham
George Innes
Harold Innocent

Brian Jackson
Gordon Jackson
Frederick Jaeger
Lawrence James
Robert James
Jerry Jardin
Stanley Jay
Colin Jeavons
Peter Jeffrey
Margo Jenkins
Peter Jesson
Reginald Jessup
Jimmy Jewel
Edward Jewesbury
William Job
Mervyn Johns
Stratford Johns
Bari Johnson
Griffiths Jones
Hayden Jones
Jacqueline Jones
Joanna Jones
Langton Jones
Norman Jones
Peter Jones
Yootha Joyce
John Junkin

Harold Kaskett
Maurice Kaufman
Patrick Kavanagh
Bernard Kay
Sylvia Kay
Barry Keegan
Kenneth Keeling
Andrew Keir
Penelope Keith
Clare Kelly
Edward Kelsey
Tom Kempinski
Bryan Kendrick
David Kernan
Annette Kerr
James Kerry
Marjorie Keys
John Kidd
Diana King
Roy Kinnear
Teddy Kiss
Richard Klee
Frida Knorr
Burt Kwouk
Thomas Kyffin

Ronald Lacey
Simon Lack
Alan Lake
Charles Lamb
Jack Lambert
Duncan Lamont
Dinsdale Landen
Marry Landis
Avice Landon
Terence Langdon
Sylvia Langough
David Langton
Robert Lankesheer
Philip Latham
Michael Latimer
Andrew Laurence
John Laurie
Jon Lauriemore
Delphi Lawrence
Sarah Lawson
Geoff L'cise
John Le Mesurier
Christopher Lee
The Dave Lee Trio
John Lee
Penelope Lee
Robert Lee
Richard Leech
Michelle Lees
Leggo
Laurie Leigh
Ronald Leigh-Hunt
Tate Leinkow
Valerie Leon
Humphrey Lestoog
Barry Letts
Philip Levene
Mark Lewin
Gillian Lewis
Rhonda Lewis
Albert Lieven
Jennie Linden
Helen Lindsay
Barry Lineham
Barry Lieneman
Yu Ling
Moira Lister
George Little
Jeremy Lloyd
Sue Lloyd
Suzanne Lloyd
Charles Lloyd-Pack
Philip Locke
David Lodge
Terence Lodge
Michael Logan
Mathew Long
Enid Lorimer
Nita Lorraine
Arthur Lovegrove
Pyson Lovell
Arthur Lowe
John Lowe
Olga Lowe
William Lucas
Michael Lynch
William Lyon-Brown
Genevieve Lyons

Ray McAnnally
Eric McCain
Helena McCarthy
Neil McCarthy
John McClaren
Allan McClelland
Gillian McCutcheon
Rory McDermot
Aimi MacDonald
Alex McDonald
Henry McGee
Jack McGowan
Oliver MacGreevy
Maria Machado
Ellen McIntosh
Fulton Mackay
T P McKenna
Michael McKevitt
Peter Mackiel
Alan MacNaughton
Duncan Macrae
Michael McStay
Peter Madden
Philip Madoc
Patrick Magee
Frank Maher
Terry Maidment
Marne Maitland
Andreas Malandrinos
Alex Mango
Hugh Manning
Howard Marion-Crawford
Marcella Markham
William Marlow
Nina Marriott
Matti Marseilles
Gary Marsh
Reginald Marsh
Peggy Marshall
Bryan Marshall
Neville Marten
Martina Martin
Francis Matthews
Mollie Maureen
James Maxwell
Roger Maxwell
Sarah Maxwell
Ronald Mayer
Ferdy Mayne
Murray Mayne
Dan Meaden
Stanley Meadows
Olive Melbourne
Michael Mellinger
Murray Melvin
Mary Merral
George Merrit
Jane Merrow
Ralph Michael
Frank Middlemas
Robert Mill
Mandy Miller
Bettine Milne
Barry Milton
Isa Miranda
Warren Mitchell
June Monkhouse
Phillippe Monnett
Richard Montez
Ron Moody
John Moore
Charles Morgan
Garfield Morgan
Donald Morley
Andre Morrell
David Morrell
Artho Morris
Aubrey Morris
Robert Morris
Wolfe Morris
Philip Mosca
Bryan Mossley
Hugh Maxley
Patrick Mower
Michael Moyer
Daniel Moynihan
Douglas Muir
Gillian Muir
Declan Mulholland
Robert Mull
Mariku Munn
George Murcell
Arnold Murle
Brian Murphy
June Murphy
Elisabeth Murray
Valentine Mussetti

Bill Nagy
Margaret Neale
Herbert Nelson
Sally Nesbitt
David Nettham
John Nettleton
Derek Newark
Anthony Newlands
Anthony Nicholls
Nora Nicholson
Michael Nightingale
Ralph Nosset

Simon Oates
Ian Ogilvy
Frank Olegario
April Olrich
Kate O'Mara
Zorenah Osborn
Brian Oulton
Richard Owens

Nicola Pagett
Louise Pajo
Jackie Pallo
Bert Palmer
Geoffrey Palmer
Julie Panle
Malou Pantera
Judy Parfitt
Cecil Parker
Rhonda Parker
Ken Parry
George Pastell
Roy Patrick

Lee Patterson
Lisa Peake
Michael Peake
Jacqueline Pearce
Ronald Pember
Arthur Pentelow
Morris Perry
Frederick Persley
Jon Pertwee
Richard Pescud
Frank Peters
Redmond Phillip
Conrad Phillips
John Phillips
Robin Phillips
Gordon Phillott
Donald Pickering
Norman Pitt
Victor Platt
Terry Plummer
Steve Plytus
Eric Pohlmann
Christine Pollen
John Potter-Davison
Denny Powell
Nosher Powell
George Pravda
Dennis Price
Hilary Pritchard
Reg Pritchard
Noel Purcell

Anna Quayle
Dennis Quigley
Jeffrey Quigley
Godfrey Quigley

Ronald Radd
Charlotte Rampling
Louise Ramsay
Henry Rayner
Corin Redgrave
Liam Redmond
Moira Redmond
Geoffrey Reed
Tracey Reed
Angharad Rees
Amanda Reeves
Kynaston Reeves
Naja Regin
Trevor Reid
Dora Reisser
Robert Reitty
Cyril Renison
Peter Reynolds
Aubrey Richards
David Richards
Terry Richards
Edwin Richfield
Arnold Ridley
Graham Rigby
John Ringham
Colin Rix

Michael Robins
Christine Roberts
Ewan Roberts
Elisabeth Robillard
Sheila Robins
Cardew Robinson
Douglas Robinson
Joe Robinson
Neil Robinson
George Roderick
Jack Rodney
Anthony Rogers
Doris Rogers
Ilona Rogers
Mitzi Rogers
Jean Roland
Guy Rolfe
Jon Rollason
Gordon Rollings
John Ronane
Edina Ronay
Andrew Roper
Alec Ross
Harry Ross
Phillip Ross
Leonard Rossiter
George Roubicek
Reed de Rouen
Patty Rowlands
Alan Roye
Anthony Roye
John Ruddick
Nigel Ruleout
Geoffrey Russell
Iris Russell
Malcolm Russell
Robert Russell
Ronald Russell
Bernice Russin
Anne Rutter
Madge Ryan
Anne Rye
Douglas Rye

Anthony Sagar
Peter Sallis
Terence Salt
Leslie Sands
Robert Sansome
Michael Sarne
Valerie Saruff
John Savident
Norman Scace
Frederick Schiller
Alex Scott
Harold Scott
John Murray Scott
John Scott
Steven Scott
Angela Scoular
Alison Seebohm
Johnny Sekka
Tony Selby
Elizabeth Sellars

Charlotte Selwin
George Selwin
Bernard Severn
Athene Seyler
Harry Shacklock
Ian Shand
John Sharp
Christine Shaw
Dennis Shaw
Willie Shearer
Nicole Shelby
Barbara Shelley
Carole Shelley
Frank Shelley
Deanna Shendery
Anthony Shepherd
Pauline Shepherd
Yvonne Shima
Bill Shino
Frank Siemen
Gerald Sim
Campbell Singer
Astor Sklair
Patsy Smart
Nicholas Smith
Sally Smith
Jayne Sofiano
Julian Sommers
Henry Soskin
Edward de Souza
Pat Spencer
Neil Stacy
Henry Stamper
John Standing
Valerie Stanton
Paul Stassino
Tony Steedman
Peter Stephens
Jeanette Sterke
Dorina Stevens
Julie Stevens
Ronnie Stevens
Monica Stevens
Jack Stewart
Roy Stewart
Nigel Stock
John Stone
Philip Stone
Kevin Stoney
John Stratton
Melissa Stribling
Virginia Stride
Veronica Strong
John Sulew
Didi Sullivan
Sean Sullivan
David Sumner
Geoffrey Sumner
Donald Sutherland
David Sutton
Dudley Sutton
William Swan
Peter Swanick
Walter Swash
David Swift

Ann Sydney
Hira Talfrey
Donald Tandy
John Tate
Grant Taylor
Malcolm Taylor
Rocky Taylor
Leon Thau
John Thaw
June Thody
Peter Thomas
Talfryn Thomas
Eric Thompson
Daniel Thorndyke
Angela Thorne
Frank Thornton
Richard Thorpe
Charles Tingwell
Ann Tirard
Robin Tolhurst
Harry Tomb
Toke Townley
Susan Travers
Frederick Treves
Ruth Trouncer
Michael Trubshawe
Michael Turner
Yolanda Turner
Meier Tzelniker

Edward Underdown
Robert Urquhart

Anthony Valentine
Valerie Van Ost
Brian Vaughan
Peter Vaughan
Wanda Ventham
Hugo de Vernier
Richard Vernon
James Villiers
John Vyvyan

Joanna Wake
Danvers Walker
Bill Wallis
Desmond Walter-Ellis
Thorley Walters
Carole Ward
Dervis Ward
Haydyn Ward
Michael Ward
Pamela Wardell
Richard Warner
Barry Warren
Kenneth Warren
Kenneth J Warren
Gary Watson
Jack Watson
Moray Watson
Richard Wattis
Gwendoline Watts

David Webb
Donald Webster
Joy Webster
Robin Wentworth
Patrick Westwood
Alan Wheatley
Lionel Wheeler
Carole White
Reg Whitehead
Geoffrey Whithead
Gordon Whiting
Margaret Whiting
Paul Whitsun-Jones
Brian Wilde
Collette Wilde
William Wild
Theodore Wilheim
Brook Williams
Alister Williamson
Anneke Wills
Douglas Wilmer
Barry Wilsher
Jerome Willis
Ian Wilson
Neil Wilson
Ronald Wilson
Frank Windsor
Vic Wise
Francis de Wolff
Hilary Wontner
Jennifer Wood
John Wood
Joy Wood
Terence Woodfield
Catherine Woodville
John Woodvine
Eric Wolfe
Jack Woolgar
Tony Wright
Anthea Wyndham
Peter Wyngarde
Michael Wynne
Norman Wynne

Terry Yorke
Eric Young
Jeremy Young
Robert Young

Peter Zander

ANSWERS TO SUBTITLE ARRANGEMENTS

To rearrange the story titles and subtitles into the correct order follow the guide below. The correct subtitle to episode **1** has been placed alongside episode **22,** and so on . . .

1-22	11-11	21-21	31-16	41-38
2-35	12-30	22- 7	32-24	42-12
3- 3	13-36	23-15	33-18	43-43
4-42	14-14	24-23	34-34	44-13
5- 5	15-29	25-47	35-17	45- 4
6- 9	16-26	26-28	36-33	46-25
7- 2	17-10	27-27	37-37	47-45
8-41	18-31	28-32	38- 1	48-20
9-49	19-19	29-39	39-48	49-40
10-46	20-6	30- 8	40-44	50-50

CAPTIONS TO PAGES 96 - 103

Page 96. In *A Surfeit of H_2O* Diana Rigg was seen for the one and only time in this dramatic PVC trouser suit designed by John Bates.

Page 97. Emma and Steed discover that even pussies can be nasty in this scene from *The Hidden Tiger.* Purr-haps they are biting off more than they can chew?

Page 98 (top). Steed seems to think the situation amusing as he comes to release Emma from the dentist's chair in *The Hour That Never Was.*

Page 98 (bottom). In *Something Nasty in the Nursery* could Sir George Collins (Patrick Newell) be dreaming about playing 'Mother'?

Page 99 (top). Steed makes an unorthodox entry into Unwin's flat in *You Have Just Been Murdered.*

Page 99 (bottom). Emma surveys her defeated opponent after a rousing fight throughout the corridors of *Castle De'ath.*

Page 100 (top). Steed finds Emma being held in a cell on a disused floor of the Chessman Hotel in *Room Without a View.*

Page 100 (bottom). In *Mission Highly Improbable* a 'miniaturised' Emma poses beside a framed photograph on the giant mock-up desk specially designed for this story.

Page 101. Reed (Patrick Allen) forces Emma to an underground chamber hidden beneath the thirteenth green in *The 13th Hole.*

Page 102 (top). Sir Lexius Cray (Nigel Green) agrees to meet Emma in a rather strange rendezvous – on the snow-clad slopes of a mountain – in *The Winged Avenger.*

Page 102 (bottom). A touch of death for Emma in *The Positive Negative Man.*

***Steed joins the Navy in* Traitor in Zebra.**

And so the story ends, or does it? Even as I sign off, news has reached me that a new series of the Avengers (emphasis on the *new*) is being discussed to a very advanced stage. Book Three. Who knows?

Dave Rogers